VIXEN

**Forbidden Pleasures Series,
Book 1**

Jade Lee

ARE YOU SIGNED UP FOR DRAGONBLADE'S BLOG?

You'll get the latest news and information on exclusive giveaways, exclusive excerpts, coming releases, sales, free books, cover reveals and more.

Check out our complete list of authors, too!

No spam, no junk. That's a promise!

Sign Up Here

www.dragonbladepublishing.com

Dearest Reader;

Thank you for your support of a small press. At Dragonblade Publishing, we strive to bring you the highest quality Historical Romance from some of the best authors in the business. Without your support, there is no 'us', so we sincerely hope you adore these stories and find some new favorite authors along the way.

Happy Reading!

CEO, Dragonblade Publishing

Additional Dragonblade books by Author Jade Lee

Forbidden Pleasures Series
Vixen (Book 1)

Lords of the Masquerade Series
Lord Lucifer (Book 1)
Lord Satyr (Book 2)
Lord Ares (Book 3)
Lord Scot (Book 4)
Lady Scot (Book 5)
Almost a Scot (Book 6)

The Lyon's Den Series
Into the Lyon's Den
Lyon Hearted

CHAPTER ONE

IT WAS LATE afternoon when Zhi Hao arrived in Peking, and well past dark when he found his way to what he hoped was Master Gao's home. But one look at the marker in front of the huge compound told him he was in the wrong place. The address he'd been given was clearly the estate of the Song family. And if the size of the walls were any indication, the Songs were very important people.

The person Zhi Hao sought—Master Gao—was a lowly instructor for men seeking to pass the imperial exam.

Fortunately, he still might be in the right place. Every major family had an attached home for a tutor. Likely, Master Gao had instructed the Song family boys until they grew of age, and now—to supplement his income—he took in other students.

Zhi Hao was likely one of dozens of men who had sought out Master Gao's help over the years. Like them, Zhi Hao's entire future rested upon the slim chance that he could pass the exam, and therefore get a good appointment as a magistrate or better.

Unlike some of them, Zhi Hao was determined to do anything it took to pass. It was the only way he could uphold his family honor and repay his parents for the crippling cost of his education. Plus, his sisters needed dowries.

But all that hope was in vain if he couldn't find Master Gao.

And so he walked—rather, he trudged—along the Song family compound until he found a door in the wall along the street. This would be where deliveries came. Perhaps someone here knew where he could find Master Gao.

His knock was not answered. Neither was his second polite bang on the wooden door. Finally, weariness overcame him.

"Master Gao!" he called. "Master Gao, it is Ko Zhi Hao! I am your newest student come from a very long way to learn from your greatness."

Nothing.

Damn it, now what was he supposed to do?

He banged again with his whole fist.

"Master Gao!"

"He can't hear you. He's in the back drinking."

Zhi looked around, wondering at the female voice. He couldn't find it, but that wasn't surprising. The walls were high, the moon was waning, and the garden inside the walls appeared to be lush.

"Up here."

He tilted his head, scanning the top of the wall until his gaze landed on a bright face with accented eyes. A girl, obviously, but one who wore makeup. That meant she was not a servant. And yet what would the Song daughter be doing up on the wall?

"Hello. I am Ko Zhi—"

"I heard. Master Gao is in the back." She leaned forward, and he saw a flash of a silk dress as she pointed down the street. "Go down there and around the corner. You'll have to walk for a minute or two, but eventually, there's a gate into the back. He never locks it. You'll find him there."

"Thank you," he said, without looking to where she directed him. He was more interested in her. "How are you up so high?"

She laughed and then did something so shocking, he quickly revised his opinion of her identity. Grabbing hold of a thick tree branch, she neatly hauled herself up onto the stone wall. It was clearly wide enough to walk, and she did so with light steps, balancing upon thin slippers.

This could not be the Song daughter. No wealthy virgin of status would dare expose her trim ankles, much less allow her skirt to billow open with her movements. Not with a strange man standing beneath her.

She had to be someone else, perhaps a maid with a wild streak. One who wore her mistress's cast-off gowns and slippers.

It was possible, he supposed.

But that was all to the good. As a lowly student, he wouldn't be allowed to meet the Song daughter, but a maid was well within his reach. He wouldn't mind a few pleasant moments with her between his studies. A man couldn't live on Confucian texts alone, now could he?

"How far can you walk on the wall?" he asked. "Can you show me the door?"

"If you cannot follow simple directions, you will fail at the exam."

He winced. That, of course, was his abiding nightmare. His family had put everything into his education, but less than one percent of applicants passed and most of them were from wealthy families with ties to the Imperial Court. He, on the other hand, came from a family of artisans. They were famous porcelain makers in the south, but that had little sway in Peking and even less at the imperial court.

"I can follow directions," he said. "But perhaps I would like to keep talking to you."

She slanted him a look, then did a beautiful spin on the wall. With her arms raised like that, she appeared like an angel in the moonlight. One with ribbons of silk swirling around her.

But then she stopped and with a laugh, she fell off the wall.

He jolted and cried out in alarm. She'd fallen on the inside of the garden where he couldn't get to. Damn it, she could be hurt!

Then he heard her trilling laughter and knew she'd tricked him.

"Around the corner, silly student."

"Trickster!" he accused.

That just made her laugh harder. He grumbled in response, but he was smiling as he began to walk. Eventually, he made it to the back gate. There, he found a lovely garden behind a modest home. To his left was another thick wall, but ahead, slumped in a chair, was a man he guessed to be his teacher.

He dropped his pack to the ground, taking a moment to breathe in the evening air. He smelled pollen from the spring garden next door, tobacco from his teacher, and the spice of good food somewhere inside Master Gao's home.

His stomach rumbled. He had precious few coins to keep him alive until his appointment, assuming he passed the exam. He needed to guard every one, and so meals had been sparse.

But first, he had to greet his new teacher. And since the sound of his pack dropping on the ground hadn't roused the man, he needed to be louder.

He moved in front of his teacher, then prostrated himself on the ground in a kowtow. From his place there, he spoke as loudly as he dared.

"Master Gao! I am Ko Zhi Hao, come to learn from your greatness."

The man jolted, starting awake as he regained consciousness. Zhi Hao didn't straighten up. He remained at the man's feet and waited to be noticed.

It didn't take long. The man kicked him—lightly—with his foot.

"Who are you to intrude on my private rest?"

For the third time that night, Zhi Hao repeated his greeting. "I am Ko Zhi Hao, come to learn from your greatness."

The master snorted and kicked him again. Not hard, but just enough to force Zhi Hao to lift up some. He kept his head lowered in respect though the position was awkward.

"Name?"

"Ko Zhi Hao."

"Who was your teacher?"

Zhi rattled off all the things he had studied and with whom. It was a long list. His family could not afford to have a live-in tutor, but had used a steady stream of travelling teachers who would visit regularly.

He ended his resume by offering up several letters of recommendation that extolled his own brilliance and layered flattery upon Master Gao by begging for the man's indulgence in teaching so lowly a student.

It was a mixed bag of statements and one that did not fool Master Gao. But it was also customary, and the man had been warned of a new student's arrival. At least, Zhi Hao hoped the letter had reached his new master before now.

"Huh," the man finally grunted. "Get up. Let me get a look at you."

Zhi Hao did as he was bid, lifting up until he rested on his knees.

Master Gao huffed out a long breath. "I'm too tired to question you tonight. If you have come this far, you had best know more than the classics. I shall require you to think and to write your ideas clearly."

"Yes, master."

"And study! Day and night, you shall have no respite. The exam is a few weeks away. That's not enough time to prepare you, but I will do my best."

He held out his hand for his fee. Zhi Hao dropped most of his coins into the man's palm. The man looked, counted, and quickly pocketed them all. Then he did something surprising.

He squatted down until he was eye to eye with Zhi Hao. "I have taught many smart men. I have instructed them in the things they needed to know, and I saw their minds blossom with knowledge."

"Yes, Master—"

"They all failed the exam!" the master bellowed.

Zhi Hao looked up, startled. "Failed?"

"Yes. And do you know why? They were brilliant, capable boys, and all from better families than you."

"Why then?" he whispered.

"Women."

"What?"

The man straightened to his full height and then spit sideways into the shrubbery. "Women," he repeated with disgust. "A horny boy cannot study. And he certainly cannot think."

Zhi Hao thought of the woman dancing along the stone wall and felt his body heat. Well hell. He needed to get her out of his thoughts now.

"I do not know if they were truly girls. I have a feeling they were fox spirits, intent on stealing chi. The girls all disappeared afterwards. Not a one stayed after they failed the exam. They had to be Fox Spirits. It's the only answer."

"What?"

The man whipped a dismissive hand in Zhi Hao's direction. "I am drunk," he growled. "But the vixens are real, and they will steal your mind from you. They will eat your power, and then you will fail at everything in life. Do you know why?"

He didn't know anything about what Master Gao was saying. Fox Spirits? Vixens? He'd heard of these things, of course. The country was filled with myths of such creatures. But he'd never met a man of education who believed in them.

"Why?"

"Because you will have given away all your power to a demon!"

Master Gao stared at Zhi Hao, as if measuring his determination...and his worth. Zhi Hao had no choice but to stare back, completely baffled by the man's raving. In the end, his new master grumbled as he turned away.

"Do nothing—think nothing—about women," he said. Then he paused and pointed to a door just inside the house. "Your bedroom's there. Don't wake me in the morning."

LING XIN LEAPED down from the wall, smiling as she went.

Fox spirits! Vixens! Master Gao was funny when he was drunk. And the look on his new student's face when the man realized his teacher believed in such nonsense? It was hilarious. Ko Zhi Hao's jaw had dropped in shock. He didn't know that when sober, Master Gao was a formidable teacher. But drunk? Well, he was prone to all sorts of ramblings.

Ling Xin hummed softly to herself, letting her thoughts wander. The new student was a handsome man. He had a sense of humor too, which was always attractive. She wondered what else he was like. Would he be one to moan and groan in his studies or find an excuse to dally with the tea maids down the road.

Over the years, Ling Xin had spied on all Master Gao's students, even her own brothers. Of course she had. There was no other entertainment for the eldest daughter of an earl (bo jue). If she had to spend her days learning poetry and practicing the Confucian virtues, at least she could have some fun in the evenings. As long as she stayed inside the walls, she was safe.

Or so she told herself. In truth, if her mother ever found out she regularly walked on top of the garden walls, she would be locked in chains in her own bedroom.

"Ling Xin! Where are you?" Her cousin Li Fei, who had recently come to live with them, called out for her.

"Right here," she responded. "Why are you up so late?"

"I've come to see you, of course. Were you walking the walls again?"

"Yes." She had no fear of admitting her favorite pastime to Li Fei. The two of them had spent a summer two years ago doing exactly that. Except Li Fei had been bold enough to escape into the city a few times. As the older cousin, Li Fei was daring in a way Ling Xin wished she could be. She'd never risk leaving her family home by herself. But her cousin had been raised in the north. She had skills and a daring soul.

Li Fei had wandered around Peking six times that summer. And when she'd returned home, she and Ling Xin had whispered together of what she'd seen and done while out and about.

Except her cousin was no longer so bold. Tonight—and every night since arriving this spring—Li Fei had been more restrained. As if something heavy bore her down.

"Master Gao has a new student," Ling Xin said hoping to spark a gleam of interest in her cousin.

It worked. "Really? You saw him?"

"I was watching on the front wall to see if anything interesting would come down the street." She grinned. "And someone did!"

"Did Master Gao make him kowtow?"

Ling Xin nodded. She had a favorite hiding spot on every wall of their home, but the one over Master Gao's back garden was the best. There was even a dark alcove in the tree branches where she had spent many an hour dreaming of her future as the next Empress of China.

It wasn't a vain hope. The Feast of Fertility would begin in a few weeks' time. After years of waiting, the time of choosing was nearly here. She would be one of many women vying to become empress, but her father assured her that she would be selected. He had done everything necessary to ensure her success. All she needed to do was impress the emperor, and then she would be selected.

That was what he said, but privately she wondered. Every bannered woman in the country would head to the Forbidden City with the exact same hope. Every one of them would be beautiful, cultured, and talented. How could she stand above the rest to catch the emperor's eye?

She didn't know and that worried her. But what could she do about it? Nothing. So she settled on telling Li Fei all about the new student.

"His name is Ko Zhi Hao, and he's from the south."

"How can you tell?"

"His accent. His clothes. He's bigger than most of Master Gao's students. He has muscles!"

"Muscles won't help him pass the exam. Is he smart? Do you think he has a chance?"

Ling Xin shrugged. "He just arrived. We won't know that for another night at least."

"You plan to spy on him?"

"What else is there to do?" She arched her brows at her cousin. Li Fei bit her lip, clearly thinking hard. Two years ago, she would have been over the wall already to peer in Master Gao's window. Instead, the girl knotted her hands together and frowned.

What had happened to suppress her irrepressible cousin?

"Li Fei, what happened to you—" she asked, but her cousin cut her off.

"We must find out if he is smart, discover if he has a chance at the exam."

Of course they would, mostly because Ling Xin was bored. But why was Li Fei so keen to know? "What difference does it make? One student is much the same as another."

"Think!" Li Fei huffed. "He must have some connection to the Forbidden City. It takes wealth and connections to be free to study all the time. No peasant boy can take the exam. He must work to eat."

"So what?"

"So connections are useful. Maybe he doesn't know anyone inside the Forbidden City, but there's a chance he does. Master Gao is a famous teacher. He doesn't take anyone as a student. Someone had to convince him to accept another one this close to the exam. And not just teach him but live with him, too." Li Fei touched Ling Xin's arm, squeezing it as she pulled them both to a secluded corner of the garden. "That means someone either powerful or wealthy has helped this man. When you become empress, you will need as many allies as you can find. If this student has connections, find out who they are. Maybe it will be useful. Once you're inside the Forbidden City, no one out here can help you."

Ling Xin felt her heart squeeze tight. It was so unfair that once she entered the Forbidden City, she would never be allowed outside again. And unless she was chosen as a favored concubine, she would never see her own family again. Females there were kept strictly apart.

"Explain to me again why you aren't competing?" Ling Xin pressed. "We were supposed to do this together."

Li Fei tsked as she pulled Ling Xin inside the house. "Never mind that. My fate has already been decided. I'm trying to help you become empress. Then maybe you can help me."

"How?"

"As empress, you will be able to do a lot of things. But first you must be selected."

"And you think this student can help me?"

Her cousin grinned. "It never hurts to ask. So long as you don't go over the wall, you can speak with him. Charm him. Find out everything he knows about what it is like inside the Forbidden City."

Ling Xin felt a thrill of excitement course through her body. Now, she had the perfect excuse to see more of the new student. Finally, she had someone new to talk to, instead of the same parents and servants she had seen nearly every day of her life. Plus, he wasn't only new. He was handsome and fun.

"He has to wander the back garden after dark," she said as much to herself as her cousin. "That's the only way we can talk."

"I'll make sure to keep people away," Li Fei promised. "Just don't—"

"Go over the wall. I won't."

CHAPTER TWO

I T TOOK SEVERAL days before Ling Xin could put her plan into action. Master Gao was a hard taskmaster, and he kept Ko Zhi Hao studying deep into the night. Her own studies also demanded her attention, especially her cultural talent, which was dancing. She spent most of the day practicing until her body ached and she wanted nothing more than to sleep.

But somehow, she always managed to find time to visit the garden wall. She couldn't help herself. Because late at night, Ko Zhi Hao practiced shadow fighting. After his teacher had gone to bed, the man stripped nearly naked in the back garden and began to move, as if fighting invisible enemies.

And Ling Xin couldn't keep her eyes off of him.

He was a beautiful man with big muscles and broad shoulders. And when he fought, he moved like a man in water—steady, controlled, and fluid.

Which made it all the more exciting when he struck out with startling speed. His punches, kicks, and whatever it was he did with his elbows came like a blow to her breath. She gasped every time some part of him moved. And her body tightened with desire.

"I know you're there," he said when he finished a lengthy sequence of punches.

She grinned. They had spoken several times now. Not in

great detail, but enough to start a friendship. They had exchanged names and spoken of their studies—well, mostly his studies. Thanks to her brothers, she knew the basics of a bannerman's education, and she had pressed him on his knowledge.

He had impressed her. And she thought she might have impressed him too. Most women wouldn't know a fraction of what she did.

Either way, they had passed several evenings in discussion of the classics while she kept her face hidden. And though he asked about her, he never pressed. Instead, he practiced his shadow fighting, and she watched with a crazy kind of obsession.

"How were your studies today?" he asked.

"Long. Yours?"

"The same."

He stepped into another series of moves and her mouth went dry as she watched. She needed to get closer. She wanted to feel his heat, smell his scent, and watch his eyes as his fists flew.

That was not allowed. She was a virgin destined for the Festival of Fertility in the Forbidden City, well placed to become the next Empress of China. She was purity itself or such was her parents' claim. The last thing she should do was climb higher on the stone wall between her garden and the neighboring courtyard. A pure woman would be asleep in her bedchamber, not wandering around, restless in the moonlight.

But here she was, being poked by tree branches and risking skinned knees from the rough wall. Thank goodness it was thick stone, wide enough that she could lay down flat and have no part of her body seen, assuming she kept her arms and legs close in.

"You're here earlier tonight. Are you feeling anxious about the festival?"

"Yes." Of course she was. After the Feast of Fertility, successful virgins would never leave the walled fortress of the Forbidden City again. Unsuccessful virgins would be thrown back in disgrace. Many would not be accepted back into the family, for any woman rejected by the emperor was considered impure. And no man wanted an impure wife.

Thinking about such a frightening possibility had brought her outside early tonight. Watching him distracted her from her fears.

"What about you?" she asked. "Worried about the exam?"

"Always. I do this to relax before I go back to my studies."

He'd told her that before. Still, she enjoyed simply being with him. But it was uncomfortable, too. What could she say to a man whose body fascinated her? There was no way a virginal girl could express such a thing. But she had to figure out something! If this was how she conversed with the emperor, she would be cut from the competition in the first hour!

"How do you stay so calm?" she asked. "The exam is only a few weeks away."

"I do this," he said, spinning around and delivering a high kick. Then he paused, his gaze going up to her. "I could teach you, if you like. Come down here. Let me show you."

She shrank backwards into the dark bower of her favorite tree. "You know I cannot."

"I know," he said, his tone light. He never pressured her, simply made the offer. And that patience made her like him even more.

Unable to resist, she pressed forward again. If he looked up, he would see her. Worse, she wore only her sleeping gown and a light robe. If there were a breeze, it might puff out to show much more than she intended. But she hadn't wanted to layer on more clothes now that winter was finally losing its grip on the world. She'd wanted to feel free, if a bit cold, and so she'd wandered into the garden, then up the wall, and now…

How beautiful he was! His pattern of movements had ended. He stood statue still, his chest expanding in slow inhales while she was entirely breathless. Her legs shifted awkwardly. She was kneeling, holding onto a branch above her head to keep her balance.

She was being daring, she realized. But when he stood tall like that, she wanted to stand with him. She wanted to lift her chin, square her shoulders, and let her body move the way his had.

Foolish, foolish girl. She needed to go back.

Then she heard a noise—not from him—but directly in her left ear. A low hiss accompanied the heat of a breath. She might not have noticed it except that the air was so still.

She jerked her head, thinking the movement would dispel whatever insect plagued her. Her eyes were still trained on Zhi Hao, but her movement forced her gaze to waver, and at the edge of her vision she saw something dark, with reddish black fur. And white, glowing eyes?

She jolted away, scrambling backwards as if she were on the ground. But the animal followed, hissing at her and she screamed. Except it wasn't a scream. Her breath was choked off in terror. And she wasn't on the ground. She was on the wall, and there was nowhere to go.

Then the creature lunged forward. She saw now that it was a fox, and she threw herself sideways...and toppled over on the wrong side of the wall.

This time, she only gasped. She was too focused on falling without marking her face. She could cover up scratches anywhere else, but her face would be seen by everyone.

She clutched at branches, feeling the leaves rip through her grip. There was a sting in her palm, a clatter as pebbles fell... She twisted. She had to protect her face. She stretched one hand out, but it was too late. She knew it even as—

Her descent abruptly halted. Zhi Hao—the gorgeous student—had caught her about the waist. Her legs flopped over and banged hard against the wall. It was all she could do to muffle her scream. But then she was completely bent over with his hands supporting her waist and she was on the wrong side of the wall. In the wrong garden!

She slowly straightened up while her body thrummed with heat and relief and terror. Where was that fox with the eyes and the huge teeth? Why had it seemed to attack? And how deliciously strong were his hands where they held her in place?

She was too embarrassed to answer her own questions. Instead, she began to squirm. "Watch out for the fox! I think it might be rabid."

"Where?"

She twisted to look. He was already easing his hold on her. She stretched out and touched the hard stone of the courtyard, wincing as one of her nails scraped the hard surface. Her mother would surely notice if one of her nails broke.

Then she pushed herself upright, wincing as she finally righted herself. Looking up, she saw that the fox had disappeared. There was nothing but fallen leaves to show what had happened. A lock of hair flopped into her face.

Damn, damn, damn!

Her hair was likely destroyed. There was no way to hide that from her mother, though she could claim that she'd had a bad dream and mussed it. She'd have to be very careful to pull any leaves out of it.

Her mind was running away with her. It was that or the feeling of having his arms around her body. He was sweaty, and she'd felt the slide of his slick muscles against her skin. And his scent was strong.

She turned to face him, her face burning crimson. This close, she could see just how big he was, not to mention muscled.

Seeing that she was all right, he stepped back and lowered his head in a bow.

So formal. After she'd dropped into his arms like a toppled vase.

How disappointing.

Of course, she hadn't wanted him to cry out...or take advantage of the fact that he held her so closely. Well, not a lot. He was larger than her and skilled as a fighter. He could do anything to her right now, but rather than impose his will upon her, he stepped back and bowed his head.

An honorable man.

She respected that, but she was still disappointed. Everything had happened so fast, she hadn't been able to appreciate the sensation of having his hands on her body. She shouldn't want that, she scolded herself. She was chaste. But now that she stood beside him, she wanted to touch him. What would it feel like to stroke her hands down his muscled chest?

Chiding herself for her thoughts, she smoothed her skirt so that not an inch of flesh showed and tried to smile demurely at him. As if she made a practice of falling into a man's arms.

"Thank you," she said, but her voice came out too husky. She cleared her throat. "Thank you," she repeated. "I... I thought I was going to be attacked. It was a fox."

"It's gone now," he said, his lips curved in a small smile.

Did he doubt her?

"Never mind," she said as she surveyed the wall from this side. How was she to get back up? And how could she do it with dignity, clad only in a nightgown and robe? Unfortunately, the moment she shifted her weight, she gasped and froze. The toes of her left foot shot spikes of pain up her leg. Damn, damn, damn. Had she broken them?

"Your feet are hurt?" His voice was deep but hushed, his words barely audible. He obviously realized the importance of keeping her presence a secret.

She glanced sideways at him, trying to appear calm. "Just a little," she admitted. "It'll make it hard to get back up on the wall again."

Before she had a chance to think, he leaned down and whispered in her ear. "Stay quiet." Then he swept her legs out from under her and held her braced against his chest.

She gasped, then looked deeply into his eyes. They seemed to reflect the moonlight, dark and mystical. Except for that mocking curve to his lips.

Was he laughing at her?

Yes, of course he was.

He took quick, silent steps to a wooden bench set nearby and set her down carefully. The whole thing lasted a few seconds, but every moment was burned into her mind. He was naked from the waist up, so she had settled against his chest. She'd felt his muscles press against her body, she'd smelled his scent, and she'd been surrounded by his heat. And all the while, her blood had thrummed in her ears…and pooled low in her belly.

Sweet heaven, this was wrong! She was destined for the Forbidden City! And yet, she couldn't stop herself from holding his scent in her lungs. She let her hand linger on his arm as he gently pulled back. Her cheeks were burning, but her eyes traced the expanse of his chest as he slowly crouched down in front of her. Her gaze travelled up his corded neck to the hard jut of his jaw, until she finally met him eye to eye.

She couldn't believe she was staring this long at a nearly naked man, and yet she couldn't help herself. She supposed she should avert her eyes, but again, she couldn't. And now, all she could do was sit there, still, staring at him while she wished for something she couldn't name.

"Where does it hurt?" he asked.

"What?"

"Your feet. Or is the pain higher?" He gently touched her right ankle.

Shivers went down her spine at his throaty words.

"Not there," she said as she gently pulled her right foot back. It was her left toes that ached. "It's my other foot," she said, but when he reached out to touch her, she stopped him. "Wait." She shook her head. "It's nothing." Then she looked back up at the wall. "I need to get home."

His gaze softened. "We have been speaking for nearly a week now. Surely you can wait a moment longer here. To see if your foot recovers."

She looked around, seeing Master Gao's garden from a new angle. "I have never been outside of my home before. Not alone."

"You're not alone. I'm here."

And that made it worse. And yet, she was loathe to leave.

"How did you learn to do that? To fight like that?"

He smiled. "It is something the monks do. It helps me relax sometimes so I can sleep."

"Which monks?" China had a huge variety of temples.

"Shaolin monks from the southern temple in Henan."

"You are a monk?" She couldn't believe it. Monks had bald heads and did not take the imperial exam.

He chuckled as he shook his head. "All us boys would peek over the walls. We wanted to see, just like you did. And we practiced, even though we were not taught."

She smiled. "You are too good to be untutored."

He grinned, his teeth shining white in the moonlight. "Some of us were taught. Not officially, but some of us managed to barter for lessons."

"Some of us, meaning you?"

"And a few of my friends." His face took on a distant look. "We were young, and the monk was kind. We were boys running around with too much energy. He gave us lessons. We gave him food from our kitchens."

There was information in his tale. He and his friends had kitchens, which meant they were wealthy enough to have extra food. They were boys running around without work, which meant they were supposed to be studying. So it made sense that he'd be Master Gao's newest student.

"And so you are here now, burning off energy when you should be studying."

"And you were watching me when a chaste girl should be abed."

Her head shot up, embarrassment and anger fighting for control of her words. Anger won.

"I am a chaste girl! I could not sleep. The air was too warm." That was a lie. The air was slightly chilled, but she had been restless, anxious about her upcoming presentation to the emperor. "And now I must go back."

"How?" he asked as he lifted up her hurt foot. Before she could object, he pulled off her slipper to expose her throbbing foot. He touched the biggest toe and the second. In the moonlight, the fact that they were swollen was obvious to them both.

"Are they broken?" she asked, trying not to panic. If her toes were broken, how would she dance for the emperor? Dance was her cultural talent. She couldn't paint worth a damn, her singing voice was acceptable but unremarkable. Her only real skill was dancing.

His hands cupped her foot. The heat from his palms warmed her, and her belly tightened at the sensation. Then it quivered inside her like a fluttering bird when he gently stroked her swollen skin.

"Can you move them?"

She wiggled her toes, pleased that it didn't hurt too bad.

"I think they are merely bruised."

That was good. "They should heal quickly, then," she said more to herself than him.

He gently set her foot down, but his fingers lingered. Indeed, he started to caress her ankle, his motions random and so thrilling. No man had ever touched her there and her body stilled just to memorize the feel of it.

Calloused fingers stroking over and around her ankle bone… Heavens, she was so aroused by it, she thought she might faint.

But then he abruptly squeezed her ankle. "Someone is coming!" he whispered.

What? She blinked, startled back into the here and now. And then she heard it. The sound of footsteps in the garden.

"Ling Xin? Are you out here?"

"My cousin," she whispered. Damn it, what was she going to do?

He pressed a finger to her lips, and she was panicked enough that she didn't dwell on the roughness of his skin or the heat against her mouth. Instead, she stared hard at the wall. She would have to find a way to scale it. She would—

She gasped as he swung her up in his arms. What was he doing? He couldn't lift her over the wall. Only a giant would be able to do that. Then he lifted her higher in his arms so that he could whisper into her ear.

"Did you really climb up the wall? You are that strong?"

"Yes," she whispered back, fighting the shiver that his lips caused as he tickled her ear.

"And your right foot is strong?"

"Yes."

"Then I shall help you."

He carried her over to the knotted tree that grew against the wall. It was a good climbing tree and would have been easy for her normally. But without strength in her left toes, she wasn't sure about it. Even worse, she would have to climb along the top of the wall in order to get back to her own garden. Not to mention the jump down once she got there.

It was a daunting prospect, but she had no choice. Li Fei called out again in a loud whisper.

"I know you are out here, Ling Xin! You never sleep when there is moonlight."

Truth.

Meanwhile, Ko Zhi Hao had set her hands on the lowest branch of the gnarled tree. It was large enough to support her weight if she had the strength in her arms.

With a last glance at him, she hoisted herself up easily, but now she needed some sort of foothold. She would have to swing her injured foot around somehow.

His hand caught her injured foot, providing a solid base for her weight as she scrambled to the next branch up. From there, her good foot had a place to land. She made it the rest of the way up with relative ease and was soon on top of the wall, looking back down to where he stood bathed in the moonlight.

"Thank you, Ko Zhi Hao," she whispered, loving the way his name felt on her lips.

He gave her an elegant bow that was all the more beautiful because it was done half-naked. How the moonlight made his skin glow!

From the other side of the garden, she heard her cousin's voice become angry. "Come on, Ling Xin!"

She rolled her eyes and then turned back to her own garden. Now that she was up here, she knew where she needed to go. She was still limping, but she managed to walk along the wall to her favorite hiding spot. It wasn't on Master Gao's side, and so not a good place to watch his students, but it afforded a nice view of the street. Indeed, it was where she'd first seen Zhi Hao.

She made her way there before awkwardly sitting down.

"Ling Xin, I'm getting annoyed with you," her cousin huffed.

"I'm here, horrible girl!" she whispered back, her tone teasing. She was very fond of her cousin. "Can't a girl look at the moon in peace?"

Li Fei came around a decorative boulder to stare at her in mock despair. "Have you lost your mind? Why aren't you wearing—"

"Hsss! You'll wake everyone."

"And you'll get sick, sitting there with just that thin covering." Then she lowered her voice to a low whisper. "Your father is awake. I had to find you in case he came out here." Then she pulled off her own robe above her evening dress. "Put this on," she said in a louder voice. "You must be freezing."

Not at all. She was still flushed from what had just happened. If her toes weren't still throbbing, her entire body would be on fire with excitement. Most of it still was.

"I bruised my toes climbing up here. Will you help me down?"

Li Fei snorted. "Serves you right for being so scandalous." Her voice dropped. "Did you find out anything useful?"

That he was as handsome close up as he was from above. "I've no practice talking with men other than my family. It's hard."

"That's why you need to keep doing it."

"I know. We've talked almost every night since he arrived."

"Still about his studies?" Li Fei huffed out her annoyance.

"That helps him, not you. You need to get more aggressive. He must know things about the Forbidden City. Find out if he has a contact inside. You need every scrap of information you can get."

"You're right. I'll be more aggressive tomorrow," she promised.

"Good. Now tell me everything you've discussed so far." Then she raised her voice loud enough to be overheard. "Let's see if there is any lychee left in the kitchen."

Unlikely. Father usually took those to eat while finishing his work administering finances. He was an earl, a bo jue, part of the highest level of Manchu aristocracy, and he served the emperor as a banker, distributing the kingdom's coin with meticulous detail. The keeping of those records often kept him up late at night, and her father was usually hungry when he worked.

Nevertheless, she knew there would be something in their kitchen, though Ling Xin would be scolded for eating when she should be keeping herself slender for the emperor.

With her cousin's help, she managed to climb down from the wall without further harming her toes. And then, some minutes later, they managed to sneak their way into the kitchen. It was all very innocent, and yet every cell in her body whispered that she was far from innocent anymore.

A man had held her naked foot in his hand. He had seen her bare legs when she fell and pressed his lips to her ear. By most measures, she was no longer a true virgin. She could still pass the emperor's exam for purity, of course, but in her heart—and most especially in her body—she thrummed with desire.

She was a fallen woman now, and every part of her delighted in that amazing experience. Too bad she could never do it again. The risk was too great, the penalty for being caught too severe. Girls could be killed for unwholesome acts. And Ko Zhi Hao would surely be punished.

And yet, she couldn't wait to sneak out to the wall again, if only to watch his glorious body move so beautifully in the moonlight.

CHAPTER THREE

Z HI HAO LISTENED as his beautiful neighbor found her cousin. He smiled at their teasing conversation—what little he could hear—knowing it was a sign of a happy family. The girls, at least, enjoyed each other.

It reminded him of his own home, where his sisters would poke and harass each other. Even when their fights seemed vicious to him, they always ended up as friends. And as usual, he felt a pang of longing.

No brother had teased him growing up. No sister had treated him with affection. Whenever they tried, they were hushed or sent away. He was the smart son. He was the one who would bring the Ko family into prominence. He was the one who would pass the imperial exam, become a magistrate, and bring fame and fortune to them all.

Or so his grandfather had decreed.

Zhi Hao had certainly taken advantage of that in his youth. He had taken the choice meats at the table, teased his sisters cruelly because he knew there would be no repercussions. Until the day he realized the cost of being a smart son.

Hours of study. Tutors who explained with their fists. And the steady weight of a family on the verge of starvation because all the money went to pay for his tutors.

Sure, he got to eat chicken, but if he made a mistake memorizing a Confucian classic, the disappointment in his grandmother's face burned down to his soul. And that was nothing compared to the times when his mother served him the chicken by saying, "Tonight you get meat because tomorrow you will fund your sisters' dowries."

Tomorrow, meaning after he passed the imperial exam, after he got a good appointment, and after his salary paid not only for his own food and lodging but there'd be enough coin for his sisters to marry well while his parents and grandparents lived in luxury.

It wasn't possible. No one except those in the highest levels of government could afford as much. He had done the math based on what salaries he had discovered. But he still had hope. And so he was here studying for the last month before he took the exam.

Still, he couldn't help smiling at the sound of the two women talking. Their words added a rush of family feeling to the already hot lust that was burning through him.

This wasn't the first time that a beautiful woman had stirred his loins. There had been many girls who were willing to attach themselves to him in the hopes that he would pass the exam. But all of his tutors had been adamant that women were distractions. He could marry once he passed the exam. His father had said the only women he should be thinking of were his two sisters. He needed to provide for them before he found a woman of his own.

But most difficult of all were his mother's words. Whenever his mind had wandered, whenever a pretty girl had passed by, she'd found a way to change the way he was thinking. Her blows had been sharp and painful. And then she'd remind him, "Your fortune is in your mind, not your jiji."

He could not get aroused without remembering her words. And so, he listened to the women chatter, he felt his aching erection, and he thought of home.

How he missed them. How he missed the laughter and the love that came with all the guilt.

How long had it been since he'd allowed himself to feel anything? For years now, his life had been spent in study, in memorization, and in the creation of black ink on parchment. Words from his own head, not feelings that burned through his body, gave his blood substance as it pumped, and desires that brought color to a life lived in black and white.

Now, one month from his final examination, he'd thought he was immune to the calling of his body. Need was burned away in the warrior exercises he performed by moonlight.

Then a woman quite literally fell from the sky into his arms. And suddenly, his body was alive again, his eyes saw color, and all his senses focused on a single gorgeous girl.

Her scent lingered in his mind, especially that split second when she had fallen into his arms. He could not imagine a more erotic moment, and his mouth had watered in a way that he had not felt since his adolescence.

Soon, he told himself, he would be in a position to find a wife. Soon he would have an appointment, a salary, and enough coin to support himself, his sisters, and eventually his own children.

How he wanted that, but it could not be now. First, he had to pass the exam.

He forced himself to go to bed. He climbed into his narrow pallet and thought of the girl next door. He thought of his future. And he wrapped his hand around his jiji and dreamed of the life he would have.

Soon.

IN THE MORNING, his life returned to black and white. Master Gao glared at him over a breakfast of steamed boa. Food which was not offered to Zhi Hao.

"You will have no food at the exam," the master said. "Best get used to an empty belly now."

That wasn't exactly true. Zhi Hao would have no food during

the three-day exam except what he brought with him. Since nearly all his money was given as payment to Master Gao, perhaps that truly meant he would have nothing to eat.

That meant he would need to steal whatever he could, hiding the food away until his exam was finished. He felt no guilt at this. Master Gao was supposed to supply his food. If the man forgot, then Zhi Hao was merely being proactive in obtaining it for himself.

Or so he told himself. In truth, after last night, nothing would stop him from passing the imperial exam. He needed a life in color, and the only way to get it was to become a high ranking official in the government. Soon he would see the end of this long road, and then he could think about a woman. Last night's woman, to be exact. One month more, and he could have it all.

He was so happy at the thought that Master Gao shot him a side-eyed look.

"Stop grinning like a fool. If you look like a fool, you will be graded as a fool."

"I am excited to be here," Zhi Hao responded. "Now I am assured to pass the exam."

"Don't be an idiot. Do you know how many people apply every year? And how few pass?"

He did. Less than two percent of applicants passed the exam, and every one of those failures looked just like him. Smart children whose family had poured all their riches into their boy's education. Only the sons who had parents already blessed as officials took the spots reserved for the best and the brightest. But lest the entire country revolt, there were always a few poor children who found a place among the exalted.

Zhi Hao would be one of them. He knew it for certain because he had been told as much in a dream. An angel had come to him and said he was one of the lucky ones.

It was precious little to base one's entire life on, but he hadn't been the only one who dreamed such a thing. His mother had too, on the very same night. The local soothsayer confirmed it the next day, which meant all the family money had gone into his education.

He would achieve the dream given to him by an angel! And then he would look to the girl next door.

"I am ready to learn," he repeated to Master Gao. And he was. He ignored his grumbling stomach and prepared to memorize every word the man had to say.

The master stared at him, a grumpy expression on his face.

"Your attitude is good," he intoned. "Your belief in yourself, however, is misplaced."

He sighed. He'd had one dream where an angel told him he was blessed. He'd had a thousand more nightmares where he slept through the exam and never again had the chance to prove himself. Or he began to write answers and everything came out as chicken scratches. Or he was running to the exam only to find the doors locked and all latecomers turned away.

"But perhaps you are one of the special ones," Master Gao allowed. "Tell me what you know about Mencius. Compare his beliefs to Xunzi." Then he folded his arms as he leaned back. "And then tell me what you believe and why."

And here, Zhi Hao grinned even wider. Two nights ago, Ling Xin had warned him to study Mencius. She'd said she'd heard her brothers talking about their studies when she was younger. And so, she was able to tell him that Master Gao had harsh opinions of the man as compared to Xunzi. Thanks to her, he was prepared for today's instructions. And what woman knew Mencius's name, much less was able to help him prepare his answers?

His nighttime lady impressed him. She also absorbed more and more of his thoughts which was a problem he could not afford.

"Are you listening?" Master Gao bellowed at him.

"Yes, Master Gao. You believe Xunzi had man's brutal nature correct."

"I think men are beasts if their minds are allowed to wander. Like yours is!"

"Yes, Master Gao. I will devote myself to your instruction."

He meant it. He needed to focus and not daydream about Ling Xin. One might think it useless to study beneath anyone who had failed the imperial exam—as was Master Gao's case— but those who passed were busy in governmental positions. Therefore, the only educators were the ones who failed. And indeed, this would be Zhi Hao's fate if his dreams did not come true. He would eke out a living teaching other hopeful students while his own chance had passed.

As the day wore on, Zhi Hao was berated at every turn for his lack of understanding. It didn't hurt him. It only made him more determined to not end up like the bitter, cruel Master Gao.

Fortunately, the teacher had to sleep sometime. And in the nighttime quiet, Zhi Hao waited for his reward.

CHAPTER FOUR

ZHI HAO HAD no doubt that his mischievous neighbor would visit. She had been on the wall watching him nearly every night since he arrived. He doubted one night's tumble would deter her for long. So it was that he was ready—already half-naked and exercising—when the plants above the wall began to rustle.

He moved in the flow of the steps, making sure to surreptitiously glance at the trees. Sure enough, his daring woman sat there, perched in the shadows to watch.

He kept working through his movements, allowing his grin to break through whenever his back was to her. And then he flowed into a set of punches, kicks, and jumps that had nothing to do with proper form and everything to do with impressing the girl who watched from atop the wall.

He ended right below her, leaping into position and freezing with his arms out.

When she did nothing, he looked up in mock surprise.

"Will you not fall into my arms tonight, angel?"

She snorted. "You know I am no angel."

"I know nothing of the sort. You did not give me your name." Though he had heard it. She was Song Ling Xin, the only daughter of the prominent family next door.

No fool, she slanted a hard look at him. "You heard my

cousin call my name."

He smiled. "Will you drop into my arms Ling Xin?"

"No. I should not have done that yesterday, and I have been limping around all day as punishment."

He frowned. "Did your parents find out?" That could spell disaster for them both.

She shook her head. "I would not be talking to you now if they had." She glanced over her shoulder, then back at him. "And I should not be here now, so I will not drop down to talk to you."

"Very well," he said with a sad smile. "I suppose I shall have to climb up to you."

And so he did, using a conveniently placed stone to jump high enough on the wall to grab a tree branch. It was a delicate maneuver. He'd already tried it twice before now and had fallen on his ass each time. He'd only succeeded when he'd found and moved the rock.

This time he jumped, grabbed the branch, and then swung himself up beside her. And she looked appropriately impressed.

"Are you a spirit?" she asked. "It's like you flew up here."

"You know I am not. Spirits probably smell sweeter than I do."

She took a delicate sniff, then wrinkled her nose. "It is not so bad."

"I am pleased to hear it." And even more pleased when he saw how her gaze roved over his chest. She leaned in to press lightly against his arm.

He shifted his position such that his forearm fell just below her breast. Indeed, he felt the weight of it on his arm and saw Ling Xin's cheeks flush pink. But she did not move away.

"Was that you singing this afternoon? It was beautiful. It distracted me from the essay I was writing."

"That was Li Fei. She had planned to sing for the emperor. It is her talent."

"Planned?" he said. "She will not go to the selection for empress?"

She shook her head. "She was meant to. Indeed, we were to go to the selection together, but her father changed his mind. I do not know why."

"So you are the one meant for the Forbidden City."

It wasn't a question. In truth, it was never a question. From the moment she was born a girl, her father had planned to make her the next empress. Nevertheless, she nodded.

"My father thinks I am more likely to attract the emperor's notice. Li Fei is small and fairy-like. Very attractive in her own way, but he doesn't think the emperor wants a fairy in his bed."

He could tell by her tone that she didn't fully understand what she was saying. Most aristocratic girls were not educated in the basics of copulation. They were kept isolated from the one thing they would need to know to attract a man. He thought it an unwise choice, but he was not a father.

"And this is what you want?" He tried to phrase it as a question, but he already knew the answer. Even his own sisters spent nights dreaming of becoming the new Empress of China, but they could not attend the Feast of Fertility from which the new empress would be chosen. There wasn't enough money to fund both the girls and his education. There wasn't enough left over for clothing, much less the bribes or training needed to outfit the future empress.

Clearly all the Song family money was going to this woman. And how could he blame them?

She was beautiful with her sweet moon face, bright red lips, and the timbre in her voice made a man's balls tighten. It was only when he looked in her eyes that he saw the wild streak in her. Her eyes danced with delight at things that should not attract a well-behaved woman. Things like bantering with a man while standing on a wall or ogling a man doing his martial arts forms in the moonlight. And a well-behaved woman would never risk climbing a wall with a hurt foot.

Ling Xin was a woman who liked to take chances, and that might not attract an emperor, but it certainly called to him. Every part of his body yearned to do more than look at her in the shadows.

Meanwhile, her mind seemed to be elsewhere. "I want to bring my family honor," she said, her expression and her tone abruptly flat. "And it is a great honor to become empress."

Oh my. That was not an auspicious answer, especially when spoken in that empty tone. He turned to face her more squarely, and when she did not respond, he nudged her arm much as he might his eldest sister.

"What do you really want?"

She arched her brows at him. It was a perfect empress look of disdain, and he marveled at the power in it. It didn't affect him, of course. She had tumbled into his arms last night, so he knew she was no prim miss. But he did admire the expression.

And he matched it with one of his own.

It took a while. He expected her to break first because women were always weak around him, but she did not. In the end, he had to give her something more than his stern expression.

"Come now," he coaxed. "I can tell you don't mean it. I will make you a deal. I shall tell you my secret if you share one of yours."

Her expression shifted to wariness, but he already knew she would give in. She liked being daring and what was more daring than trading secrets with a stranger?

"You first," she said.

He nodded. He had expected no less. "I have two sisters who are eligible for the Feast of Fertility."

She gasped. "What are their names? I will—"

"They are not going, and I am not sad about that."

Her expression shifted to compassion. "Are they ill-formed? I am sorry."

She actually looked sad for him, and he had to stifle his laugh. "They are both considered beautiful women, but unlike your family, we do not have the money to outfit them."

"Oh," she said, her gaze going to the neatly folded pile of his clothing. He had set it there before he began his exercises. Even from here, she could likely tell that the fabric was expensive. Also, the embroidery was exquisite because it had been done by his own mother's hand.

"That is not my secret," he said. "My secret is that I am pleased we cannot afford to send them. Life in the Forbidden City is terrible. I would not wish that on anyone."

She gaped at him, her eyes widening in shock. And well she should. What he had just said could be considered treason. But the way she hunched her shoulders told him that she had already suspected as much.

"Have you ever been in the Forbidden City?" she asked.

"No, but my uncle is a eunuch there. He is the one who pushed my family to train me for the imperial exam. He paid most of Master Gao's fee. I have learned much from him about what it is like there."

She turned, her eyes wide and her expression open. "What did he say? You must tell me. I must be prepared for what is ahead."

That was very true. "What do you know?"

She shook her head. "Nothing. Just that—"

"It is a great honor." He spoke the words for her because those were the words every proper girl said. And she obviously understood because her chin dipped in depressed agreement.

"It is a great honor," he continued, "if you are selected to become the empress. All the other candidates leave disgraced and their families are supposed to decry them as tainted."

"Not all!" she cried. "Some will become favored concubines."

"Only four will be favored. The rest will live in palaces alone, never seeing the emperor, never having the chance to bear him a child."

She looked at him, her eyes wide with hope and fear. "I'm sure that's not true," she said, though her tone told him she wondered.

"I know it is true," he countered. "Those selected will have a difficult life. Those disgraced will be lucky to marry at all. Better to never try."

"No!" she said firmly. "I am sure the unlucky girls will be accepted back into their families. It is no disgrace to be refused by the emperor. He can only select a few out of the whole country."

"Will your family take you back?" he asked, hoping her answer was yes.

She bit her lip. "They will not entertain the possibility, but I have spoken in secret to my aunt. She said I can live with them as Li Fei's adopted sister."

A good fate. Better than many. "Will you be able to marry?" Would she be able to escape the confines of the family compound to meet anyone?

Her smile was forced. "I hope so."

"I do, as well."

She was silent for a long while, then she spoke with renewed strength. "Do you not have faith in your sisters to attract the emperor's gaze? Are they not virtuous enough?"

He didn't want to answer this. It wasn't his place to enlighten her. Worse, if her family was adamant, there was nothing she could do to change her future. And yet, he could not stop himself.

"My sisters are wonderful women, virtuous and kind. And so I know they would be failures in the Forbidden City."

She jerked, obviously shocked by his statement. "But why?"

"Because virtue is not what attracts a man. And kindness will not help you in court."

She winced as she stared at her hands, but she said nothing.

"You cannot change this, can you?" he asked gently. "Your father insists?"

"He says I will become empress or I will be nothing. Not his daughter, not anyone he knows." She sighed. "He doesn't mean it so harshly. He thinks such words will motivate me to try harder, but I cannot work any harder than I am. I dance for hours every day, I study the Confucian virtues. I even write poetry, though I am terrible at it."

"And your father thinks that is what will catch the emperor's eye?"

"Certainly." She shrugged. "That and my beauty." She spoke without ego, her shrug dismissing the perfection of her face and body. And that humility was more attractive to him than the body of an angel.

He shook his head, daring to touch her arm. "Virtue is not what attracts a man. And for all that he is the King of Heaven, the emperor is still a man."

She opened her mouth to argue. Indeed, girls such as her were taught that the emperor was a kind of deity. But she had to know the truth if she was to have a chance where she was going. He was searching for a delicate way to suggest something scandalous when her mind leaped to it before he could voice it.

"What must I learn?" she asked.

She was so earnest in her expression, so beautiful a temptation, that he knew he wouldn't be able to resist. Only a worm would do what he was about to do, and he was a moral man.

No. He was a worm who pretended to be a moral man because he could not stop himself.

"I can teach you," he said slowly. "But it is not something you can tell anyone. If we are discovered, we will both be killed."

She narrowed her eyes in suspicion, and well she should. This was a dangerous game, but it was also her only hope.

"Tell me," she commanded.

His blood surged at her tone. Only a woman reared to be an empress could sound so sexy as she ordered him to obey.

"Forgive my bluntness," he said, fighting a grin.

She nodded.

"The way to attract a man is to sensually delight him. Innocence is boring. You must understand what excites the emperor, and you must become that for him in all ways."

There. He had dropped the breadcrumb, but was she daring enough to pick it up?

"How do I learn that?"

He took a deep breath. How far did he dare tempt her? How much did she know?

He looked around and listened closely. There was no one around. His master was asleep.

"Will anyone come looking for you tonight?" he asked.

She shook her head. "Even Li Fei is asleep."

"Then I will show you the most basic of truths."

She nodded. "I will tell no one."

She'd best not or they would both die—him for corrupting her, her for being corrupted.

Nevertheless, how could he refuse her when she looked so beautiful and so eager.

He adjusted his position beside her on the wall, bracing one hand on a tree branch to prevent himself from falling. Then he smiled at her.

"Do you know anything of a man? Of what makes him interested in a woman? How she can excite him?"

Ling Xin bit her lip, looking adorably intrigued. "My mother says a man is attracted by goodness. My father says my dancing will entrance everyone."

"And what do you think?"

"That there is a great deal more to learn. Otherwise, every dancer and kind soul would be overrun by lustful men."

He laughed at that. She had a logical mind and a sense of humor. That appealed to him. "Do you know what happens when you are interested in a man?"

She nodded slowly and he saw her cheeks tinge red in the moonlight, but she didn't say anything. That was not a surprise. Girls were not taught much about their own bodies, so it was left to him to say it aloud.

"Does your heart beat faster? Is there heat in your belly?"

"Yes," she whispered, and he could see the truth of it in her breathless answer.

"It is the same for a man." He gently took hold of her hand and pressed it against his chest. "Do you not hear how my heart thrums at your nearness?"

She nodded. Then he carefully pushed her hand lower. Not far enough. Not to where he throbbed for her, but low enough that she could feel his heat.

"I desire you, Ling Xin." Then he did something daring. He reached out with his other hand and stroked her cheek. Her eyes had been on his belly, but now she looked into his face. "Do you feel how heavy your breasts feel? How your lips are dry and your mouth aches to be kissed?"

She bit her lower lip and nodded. Her eyes were wide, but not with fear. She was thrilled by what he told her, excited and hungry for more. How he wanted to show her, but he could not. It was too dangerous for them both.

So he released her and leaned back against the branches of the tree.

"That is arousal," he said. "That is what you must excite in the emperor."

She looked at him a long time. She lifted her hand and slowly stroked the side of her cheek where he had touched her. And then she straightened with a look of fierce determination.

"I am not completely ignorant," she said firmly. "I have brothers."

His brows went up. She wanted something specific from him, but he could not guess what. Fortunately, she was not evasive.

"I have heard about a man's jiji. I know that men take great pleasure in it, and that a woman must make it…stand up." She paused before she said the last two words, clearly not knowing what they meant. Then her gaze dropped to the thin fabric of his pants. "I want to see it. I want to know what that means." She flashed him a coy look. "Because the emperor has one, does he not? And I must know what it looks like and how to… how to…"

"Make it explode?"

"Yes!" she exclaimed, and the relief in that one word shocked him.

"Have you been thinking about this for a while?"

She nodded.

"Ever since you saw me practice my kung fu?"

"Ever since I learned that an empress, above all things, must give the emperor a son. But whenever I asked how she was to do this, I was told that I would learn it when I was older. Well, I am older. It is less than a month before the Feast of Fertility, and still, no one will answer." Her voice took on a pleading note. "So will you show me, Ko Zhi Hao? Will you teach me how to be an empress?"

He thought her well on her way to being the female leader of China. She had the mind to understand where her knowledge was lacking and the boldness to demand answers. But what she asked for was...

Exciting.

Daring.

Absolutely not something he should do. And yet, as her eyes quietly begged him to agree, he found himself bending to her wishes. What man could refuse such earnest desire?

He took a deep breath and tried to slowly introduce her to what she wanted. "You have heard of a man's jiji. Do you know how he swells and explodes with seed?"

"Only that he does, and I shall be pregnant."

"He must explode inside you for that to happen."

Her eyes widened. "So your seed can explode now and I shall not get pregnant? And I can see it?"

His heart was beating nearly out of his throat. She had the eagerness of a child wanting to learn a new skill. But there was also a daring excitement that lighted her eyes and made his cock ache with hunger. She knew what she was doing was forbidden. They both did. And yet, she still demanded his help.

"I must see it!" she said. Then with more determination. "I must learn how to make it happen."

And so without another word, he took her hand and gently brought it to the ties of his short pants.

She was hesitant. But her fingers twitched with eagerness,

and he knew she was as eager to learn as he was to teach. Still, he cautioned her.

"I will not touch you," he said. "I will not harm you, but you must choose this. I am risking much."

"I know," she said softly. "But I will not tell. You are helping me."

Was he? Debatable. Especially as his organ swelled to near bursting. But one look at her told him that she was equally aroused. Her breasts were high and pointed, and her lips were wet where she had licked them.

She wanted what he offered, and worm that he was, he intended to take full advantage of that. But she had to make the first move. He would not have her say he forced her.

"Release my pants and you will see my male dragon, full and eager because I am a man and you are beautiful."

She looked at him as if to gauge his truthfulness. He held his expression calm, but he could not hide the way his organ bobbed in hunger though she had yet to touch him.

"Are you lying to me?" she asked in a whisper.

"No." Then he arched a brow. "You can see the evidence yourself."

She rolled her eyes. "Not about that. I know that a dragon thickens." She looked hard into his eyes. "Do you lie about this being the way to the emperor's heart?"

"It is the way to the emperor's bed."

He could see the truth of that hit her, but he also guessed that she'd been looking for a reason to do what she really wanted.

She needed no more prompting. Her fingers fell to his pants, untying the rough cord with ease. The fabric tented over his erection. He was about to say something to encourage her to uncover him, but he needn't have worried.

She pulled down the fabric and smiled as his full dragon sprang up toward her.

Cold air hit his heated flesh, and he shuddered at the sensation. He prayed that he could keep himself calm long enough to enjoy what was coming. Meanwhile, she was studying him as if he were a Confucian text.

"The emperor will be like this?" she asked.

"No doubt he will be bigger, more impressive—"

"And shoot stars of golden light from his tip. Yes, I'm sure that's true." Her tone was thick with irony. "I believe he is a man just like you."

The emperor was a great deal more than Zhi Hao could ever be, simply because he was the emperor. But Zhi Hao didn't argue. He was more interested in what she would do next.

The answer surprised him. She approached him logically, asking for direction rather than grabbing him. That proved she was smart and that she could control her impulsive nature when she wanted.

"How do I touch it?" she asked. "Do I grip it with strength? Does it prefer caresses? How—"

"Every man is different, but I think variety is what entices most men."

She nodded, her focus very intent. Then she began to explore.

He saw no more hesitation in her, but a systematic discovery—with an excruciatingly light touch—of his length and girth. If felt like being caressed by lightning. Tingle and fire wherever she touched, lingering long after she'd moved on.

It took all of his strength to keep his breath even. And then she grew bolder.

She enfolded him in her grip, and he felt each finger wrap around him in a delightful sheath. Indeed, his eyes rolled back in his head and his buttocks tightened, naturally thrusting into her hand.

"This feels good?" she asked, her voice barely above a whisper. "You like it completely covered?"

He nodded, trying to keep his sanity when pleasure wrapped around his organ.

"It is what a man feels when he is inside a woman and they make a child," he said. "He enters her and she squeezes him."

So she did exactly that, tightening her grip around him. He groaned in delight and thrust again.

"There is wetness here," she said, spreading her thumb across the crown.

His mind whited out at the sensation. And when he could think again, he saw that she was studying his face.

"Does this steal your thoughts?"

"Yes. When it is done right, a man cannot think at all."

"And the wetness?" she asked as she once again rolled her thumb over the crown.

He groaned, fighting to keep the sound inside. "That is the beginning—" he gasped. "—of my seed."

"The beginning? Not all?"

He nearly laughed at the insult. "Not all. Barely a start."

"Oh." She looked down and then back up at him. "What do I do next?"

His mind stuttered on the graphic images that flooded his brain. He wanted her tongue on his tip, he wanted her mouth encasing him, he wanted her on her back as he thrust inside her.

He said none of that because it was too sudden for her. And too much for him.

"What do you want?" he asked her, because he could not allow what he was thinking.

"I told you. I want to see you explode."

"An excellent idea," he quipped. Then he adjusted his position, leaning back against the tree. She released him as he moved and the changing sensation made his blood surge again. But he was not stable here and this position was awkward.

He abruptly lifted his leg up and over her head, leaving her sitting between his thighs. She hadn't been expecting it, so she released a muted cry as she ducked. But far from being afraid, she laughed.

"You could have hit me in the head!"

"Never."

"Hmmm," she returned. She was between his legs now,

facing him squarely. She returned to his dragon, wrapping him in the tight silk of her hand.

"What should I do?" she asked.

Everything! But he could not say what thoughts flooded his mind. He had to go slow, though his blood and his hunger surged inside him.

"Hold me and watch," he said. "I shall do what a man does between a woman's thighs. Imagine your hand is your most private place."

She frowned. "My most private…?"

How he wanted to show her! How he wanted to touch her and make her feel what he did. Instead, he tried to explain with words.

"Do you tingle? Does the flesh between your thighs grow wet?"

Her eyes widened. "Yes!"

"Imagine me there." Which was exactly what he was thinking.

It would not take long. He was at the edge of release now.

He watched her expression as he moved, seeing her excited interest. In his mind's eye, he was kissing her breasts, running his tongue over her peaks before nipping at her until she cried out. He was spreading her legs and thrusting deep into her. And she was gripping his backside, moaning beneath him.

That should have been enough to have him exploding like an adolescent boy. It was not. Because he did not know her breasts yet, had not smelled the scent of her arousal, and he certainly was not privy to her intimate places.

What he saw was her tongue, slipping between the red folds of her lips. He felt the varying strength of her grip on him. And best of all, he saw it when she grinned up at him. There was power in her expression, a realization that he was at her mercy.

His hips were thrusting into her fist, his breath was a ragged pant, and his thighs quivered with need.

"Explode," she said. "Now."

There was such command in her tone that it shocked him. No young virgin should know how to order a man's release. And yet, she did. While he plowed into her fist, those two words tipped him over the edge.

He released with a fire so hot, lightning burst behind his eyes. And he kept pumping while her fist grew slick with his seed.

"Oh!" she whispered as she watched him erupt. "Now I understand."

Did she? Doubtful. But at least she was a little more prepared.

"How long does that go on?" she asked as he continued to pump.

"Not much longer," he panted.

Then his body gave way and he slumped back against the tree trunk, letting his gaze rove over her flushed face, her pointed nipples, and the sweet nectar he imagined between her thighs.

She smiled. "How soon can you do it again?"

He chuckled as his legs flopped open wide. "Fifteen minutes or so, but you will have to encourage it. Most men need to sleep for a bit."

"Oh." She frowned, clearly thinking hard. "Do I caress it again? Is that how—"

"No, you will have to do something else. It is too sensitive right now." Though the way she was studying him seemed to bring new life into his dragon. He did love an inquisitive mind.

"Then how?"

There were so many ways to answer that. So many things he wanted to do with her.

"You must get me to kiss you."

"What? How?"

No virginal outrage in those words. Just simple curiosity. And clear excitement at doing something so daring.

He let his head drop back as he savored her eagerness. "You must make we want to take you again," he explained. "And that begins with a kiss."

"But how do I make you want to kiss me?"

The better question was how could she stop him, but he

didn't say that. He was too happy with her eagerness at the moment.

"Give me a moment to think," he said, drawing out the anticipation. Then he straightened up, seeing that there were things he had neglected.

They were both a mess. He used the edges of his pants to clean himself and her. It was crude, but he had nothing better. And while he cleaned her, he savored the refined length of her hands and the surprising strength in her fingers. He caressed her callouses, knowing that she was a refined lady who had no doubt spent years studying how to hold a brush in a way that made the most beautiful strokes.

She seemed to enjoy what he did, allowing it, despite the crudeness of the fabric.

Then she grew impatient. "How do I get the emperor to kiss me?" she pressed.

Bringing the emperor into the conversation killed the moment. He had been pretending that she wanted him.

"That is a complicated question," he said, stalling for time. "I cannot answer it—"

"You will tell me!" she said, and though there was command in her tone, there was also uncertainty. She sat in front of him with her hand wet and her cheeks flushed. She was aroused and unable to satisfy herself.

Sweet heaven, she was fascinating!

"Give me your other hand," he said. He began to rub it, using his fingers to knead into her palm. And as he worked, he pressed the back of his hand into her belly. He moved in slow circles and watched as she shifted uneasily on the wall. If the emperor did choose her, he would be a lucky man. She was ripe for erotic play, and so eager to learn.

"You must tell me," she said again as she pulled her hand back from him.

He grimaced, burning with jealousy.

"Ko Zhi Hao—" she began, but he interrupted her.

"I will kiss you if you ask. You need do nothing more tonight."

She frowned, clearly confused. "That's it?"

That was everything. She had to ask.

"That is all."

She leaned forward, her face flushed, her eyes bright in the moonlight.

"Please kiss me," she said. Her tone was breathless, her desire obvious.

"Have you ever been kissed before?"

Her eyes widened. "I could never."

Of course not. He would be her first.

"Then I shall go slow."

He leaned into her, letting their breaths mingle, and then he slowly pressed his mouth to hers.

Her lips were wet and supple. He moved gently across them, waiting until her mouth slipped open of its own accord. Then, when she did, he teased his tongue inside.

He felt her breath catch, and he waited until he could control his movements. His blood was roaring in his body, his dragon already leaping forward again.

When he finally allowed himself to slip inside, she was heaven itself. Her tongue darted forward to meet his, daring minx that she was. And as he pressed forward, she let her head drop back so he could plunder her mouth.

She tasted of hot lychee sweetness, and he would never again eat that fruit without thinking of this moment.

And then she tried to take control.

The way her tongue abruptly thrust against his shocked him. He'd thought her a shy virgin, but this was a boldness he hadn't expected. Her tongue twisted and teased his, and if they hadn't been perched on top of a rock wall, he might have risked it all to take her.

She was a wildcat.

And in that moment, he resolved that he would have her for his own.

CHAPTER FIVE

LING XIN WAS no fool. She understood that what she was doing was scandalous. Indeed, her father might truly kill her if she were caught. But she knew that this wonderful man was teaching her things she needed to know.

He was also taking advantage of her. Of course, a man wanted a girl to help his dragon roar. And she, in turn, was delighted to find that she enjoyed such a thing as well. It wasn't just learning about something so basic to men and women. She adored the thrill of it.

She was kissing a handsome man in the moonlight. She was feeling his strength pressed against her, twisting tongues and feeling her belly liquify. Oh, she wanted to feel it all! But she knew this was crazy dangerous.

So she pressed her hand against his chest, pushing him back and felt a moment of panic when he didn't move away.

And then he did.

Her breath was heaving, her heart pounding. And when he looked at her like a man about to take what she so wanted to give... Well, this was the thrill and the danger.

Thank heaven he was honorable.

"I think I have learned enough tonight," she said, her voice rough.

He gave a wry chuckle. "You have learned, that is for certain.

But it is not enough."

"It is enough for tonight," she said sternly.

He didn't argue. And she didn't run away. And because she thought him honorable, she pressed him for the truth.

"Will this truly help me catch the emperor's eye?"

Of course, a cad would lie to her and say, "Certainly!" He didn't. Instead, he shrugged. "I don't know. But it will serve you better than memorizing the Confucian virtues." Then he rubbed a hand over his face. "We are both fools to do this."

She grinned. That was the answer of an honorable man. "Thank you for the lesson," she said. Then with a quick twist, she began to scramble away. She had set up a chair for her use, and so she landed easily back in her garden despite her wounded toes.

Then she looked up to see him watching her, his face in shadow but clear enough to her eyes. "Will you come back tomorrow night?" he asked. "There is more to learn."

"There is always more to learn," she whispered back. It was not an answer. Let him wonder whether she would appear tomorrow night. She wasn't sure herself.

She waved to him as she gathered the chair and slipped as quietly as possible back into her house. As she moved, she felt her clothing brush against her sensitive breasts. She felt the liquid tension in her belly, and she ached to know more.

She was so aroused that she didn't see the lump in her bed. Not at first. Her mind was still back in the garden. But then she lifted the covers only to have that lump grumble in annoyance.

"Li Fei!" Ling Xin hissed. "What are you doing in my bed?"

"I came to talk with you, but you weren't here." Her cousin sat up and rubbed her eyes. "How was your conversation with Zhi Hao?"

Thankfully, the room was dark enough to cover her blush. "I learned that he has an uncle who is a eunuch in the Forbidden City."

Li Fei sat up with a grin. "But that's excellent! What's his name? What does he do?"

Ling Xin slipped under the covers, keeping her voice low as she spoke. "I'll ask him that tomorrow," she said.

Her cousin rolled her eyes. "What do you two talk about?" she huffed. "You were gone long enough for me to fall asleep."

A tremor of fear skated through Ling Xin's body. Li Fei could not find out what she'd done. Much as she adored her cousin, she couldn't trust that the girl would keep that big a secret. "Hush! No one can know what I'm doing."

Her cousin rolled her eyes. "I won't tell. It was my idea! But you cannot be a prim miss about this. An empress will have daggers on every side. You must learn to take what you want and not get caught!"

"I begin to fear the Forbidden City."

Li Fei huffed out a breath. "Surely you know that every position of power has enemies. Life in the Forbidden City is very different from out here. Your father must have taught you that."

"Not like you do." Not like Zhi Hao did. What they told her frightened her, and she began to fear her future.

"An empress must be bold. And she must be wary of those who would hurt her. You must learn to take advantage where you can and hide when you cannot."

Ling Xin studied her cousin with new eyes. Two years ago, Li Fei had giggled about laborers with their muscled bodies dripping sweat. The two of them had whispered about what men and women did in bedrooms and wondered what it would be like when it was their turn.

But now Li Fei spoke about daggers and deception as if it were a matter of course. During the day, she practiced singing and discussed the merits of different cosmetics. It was as though the girl had no more interest in men and was completely focused on competing for the emperor's hand. And yet, she already knew she would not be the one to go.

It made no sense.

"Did something happen last year?" she abruptly asked her cousin.

Li Fei pulled back. "What? No! Why would you ask that?" Her outrage was overdone. The girl was not as good at deception as she thought.

Ling Xin leaned forward, her voice dropping into a barely audible whisper. "You can trust me. I won't say anything. You know all my secrets." It was a lie. She would take what she had done this night to her grave.

But her cousin dismissed her with a wave. "You are too good to have secrets. Watching a man sweat in the moonlight is not so terrible a thing." She slanted her cousin a look. "Unless you were doing something else?"

"Something else!" Ling Xin exclaimed. "There is nothing else to do when we are trapped inside all day singing or reading poetry. I am sick to death of this life."

"Which is why I asked the question." Her cousin rolled closer, until they were nearly nose to nose. She'd always had the patience of a stalking cat. Her voice dropped to a serious tone. "What were you doing out there?"

"I was thinking," Ling Xin lied. The last thing she'd been doing was thinking. And yet, the word came out nonetheless. "Day after day, we are taught the Confucian virtues. Every girl set before the emperor will be virtuous and beautiful."

"Not every girl is beautiful."

"But every girl set before the emperor will be."

Li Fei nodded. They both knew it was true.

"So I must find a way to be different. Some way that will pique his interest."

"That is why we are taught how to converse."

Ling Xin nearly gagged. "Ugh. More poetry and the beauty of flowers. Even mother is bored by those topics."

Li Fei flopped onto her back. "What are you thinking?"

Ling Xin sat back on the bed so that she was leaning back against the wall. "What if we need to know how to be courtesans?"

Her cousin opened her mouth to argue. She was the picture

of proper outrage at the very idea. But she didn't speak. It was as if the words froze in her throat. And that was when Ling Xin knew that her cousin had indeed done something unexpected.

"Oh, Li Fei, you must tell me."

Her cousin shook her head. "It is nothing." And when Ling Xin began to object, her cousin gripped her hands. "I met a man. That is all. A man who…" She shrugged. "Well, he was very exciting."

Ling Xin bounced on the bed. "Tell me everything!"

But her cousin's expression wasn't eager. It was shadowed and sad. And she wouldn't look Ling Xin in the eye. "We were caught," she said. "That is why I am here. Did you not wonder?"

Ling Xin nodded. "I thought you had wandered to the market alone. That's what Mama said."

"I did. And then I went a great deal further." Li Fei looked away and even in shadow, Ling Xin could see that she was crying.

"What happened?" she whispered.

"I was sent here." The words sounded like a death knell. Then Li Fei shuddered. "After I proved that I was still pure."

Ling Xin bit her lip. She had heard that such an experience was awful. It would be required of her during the Feast of Fertility. All potential brides had to prove their virginity. But that wasn't the worst thing in what her cousin had said. Li Fei had said, "*We*." As in, they were both caught.

"What happened to him? To the man you were with?"

"Dead."

The word was spoken so quickly that Ling Xin barely heard it. Her heart throbbed painfully in her throat. But it couldn't be true. Her uncle was not a violent man.

"Are you sure?" she asked.

Li Fei nodded. "Father showed me the bloody clothes. Then he brought me here. He did not speak one word to me the entire trip. It was as though I was not his daughter anymore. Maybe not even a person."

"No!" Ling Xin cried. "He loves you still. You are his daughter."

Li Fei shook her head. "You judge my father by your own. It is different in the northern villages. We are by nature more violent."

"More cruel, you mean."

Li Fei shrugged. "It is one and the same."

Ling Xin gently wrapped her cousin in her arms. The girl was openly weeping now, though she made no sound.

"Did you love him?" she asked.

The tears flowed harder then, quickly drenching her thin night dress. Ling Xin took that to mean that yes, the girl had been in love. It was a long time before either of them spoke again. And when they did, it was because Ling Xin's mind was racing with the risks she was taking. After all, it sounded as if her cousin hadn't undressed a man or stroked his dragon, and still her man was dead and she had been banished here.

"Your father sent you here," she finally said. "To do what?"

Li Fei pulled herself together, though it took some time. Eventually she spoke, though her voice was shaky. "Father would not send me to the emperor. He said I was disgraced, and he would not play the emperor false."

"But then—"

"Your father is to find me a husband here where no one knows me. He gave your father ten pieces of jade. He told him to marry me to whomever can stand the stench. He will hear no more of me."

Ling Xin was shocked that her uncle could be so harsh. She had been away at a dancing lesson when her cousin had arrived at their home, and she'd been told nothing except that Li Fei was here to find a husband. Now, she understood why the girl had seemed so depressed.

"I am so sorry," she said, and she meant it with her whole heart. "If I could change it, I would."

"Just do not make my mistake," Li Fei said. "Look all you want over the wall, talk to him and find out what he knows, but do not go further."

Ling Xin wanted to argue, simply because she had already risked more than a simple look. Of course, she had heard tales of fathers killing unlucky suitors. Of girls who strayed when they shouldn't have, and had paid a horrible price. But her father loved her. He would beat her, but he would not…

Marry her off to the lowest bannerman simply to be rid of her taint?

Yes, he might very well do that. Just like her uncle, her father would not risk insulting the emperor with an impure daughter.

"But how am I to entice the emperor?" she finally asked, the words an anguished whisper. And when her cousin looked at her, she struggled to explain, repeating Zhi Hao's words. "He is a man, and no man wants virtue in his bed."

Her cousin shook her head. "I do not know. I only know the cost of becoming impure."

Ling Xin huffed. "You aren't impure. You took a walk."

"And a kiss," Li Fei whispered. "Such a wonderful kiss."

So there had been more. "Tell me about it," she urged. "Tell me everything!"

Li Fei shook her head. "There is no way to describe it. Except that I never wanted it to end."

That told her nothing. When Zhi Hao had kissed her, she hadn't wanted it to end either. But that wasn't love. That was experimentation. That was excitement and learning the ways of seduction.

"I think that is the way with love," continued Li Fei. "One touch, and one is desperate for more. Every moment, every look, every…thing." Li Fei sighed. "I lost all sense because I was in love. It made me careless. I didn't think things through."

"I won't fall in love," Ling Xin vowed. "And I'm very careful." That was debatable, but she renewed her determination to stay vigilant.

"It's hard to think when one's heart is beating as if for the first time," Li Fei said.

Ling Xin's heart was still beating hard, and just the memory of his touch made her toes curl in delight. But that wasn't love. That was the restlessness she always felt surfacing when there was something new to learn, something exciting to discover. She knew this feeling well, though it was certainly more intense now than ever before. Either way, she wasn't in love. And so, she reasoned, it was safe for her to continue. So long as she was very careful not to get caught.

Which was, frankly, a childish and ridiculous thought.

She was fooling herself. She knew it. And so, before she risked everything—including her life—on midnight dalliances, she had to speak to the most logical, practical, and plain-speaking person she knew. Her mother.

CHAPTER SIX

L ING XIN HAD a great deal to think about come morning. It
was clear she was walking a dangerous path with Zhi Hao,
but sometimes dangerous paths were necessary. Especially if one
dared to become empress.

And so she sought out her mother, the one person she knew
had the most common sense.

The lady was in her solar, rolling bandages for the hospital.
She also mixed medicinal salves according to her brother's
recipes. He ran the most prestigious apothecary in Peking.
Indeed, Mama's family had been associated with medicine and
healing arts for generations.

Except for her mother, of course, who rolled bandages and
mixed salves in her spare time because she was the wife of an
important court official. And because the lady was squeamish
when treating the ill. Whenever Ling Xin or her brothers had
been ill, their nanny was the one who had tended them. At most,
their mother would speak to them from the door rather than step
inside the sickroom.

"Good morning mother," Ling Xin said as she entered the
solar.

"Good morning dear. Have you finished your dance practice
already?"

Ling Xin sighed dramatically. "I fear I have been working too hard. My ankle hurts, so I decided to rest it today."

"Wise of you," her mother answered without looking up. "But what of your voice? I have not heard any singing. You must not lose the opportunity to learn from Li Fei. She has a beautiful singing style. And, you know, singing can be heard from a distance. If the emperor does not see you dance, perhaps he can hear you sing."

"An excellent idea," she said, though privately, she wondered if the emperor's living space would be anywhere near the virgins who awaited his pleasure. If it was, then there would be dozens of virgins trying to sing for his attention.

But of course, she didn't know if this was true. She didn't know much of anything about what happened in the Forbidden City. And that was the whole problem.

"Mother, I have been thinking," she said as she sat down and started rolling bandages.

The lady heaved a loud sigh. "And now you shall ask me something inappropriate." The lady shook her head. "You cannot do such things in front of the emperor. No one wants to hear your bizarre thoughts."

Ling Xin tried not to be hurt by that statement. On one hand, her mother had often admonished her for not thinking before acting. And now she was supposed to stop thinking? Or perhaps just stop sharing her thoughts, which was more likely.

But that did not stop her from carrying on with her questions.

"I am afraid you are correct, Mother," she said, her tone a little harsh. "But I must ask someone for guidance, and my options are limited."

"Guidance?" Her mother set down her finished bandage and looked at her. "On what topic?"

"You have set me the task of attracting the emperor—"

"And we are very proud of you for that," her mother interrupted.

Ling Xin nodded, then decided to simply say it baldly. "I do not know how to attract a man."

"You are kind, beautiful, and well versed in the Confucian virtues."

"Just like every other girl there." She touched her mother's hand. "But I need to be *more* than every other girl there."

"It is your beauty—"

"Every girl will be beautiful."

"But you—"

"Mother!" she snapped, her impatience overcoming her good sense. "I need to know how to attract a man. Don't pretend you don't understand. I have heard uncle speaking of the prostitutes who come to the hospital—"

"Do not say those words!" her mother growled. "You should not even know about them. The emperor does not want such knowledge in a wife!"

Ling Xin grimaced. "Are you sure? What is his wife except a vehicle for his child? What are his concubines for, except for that?"

Mama sniffed with all the disdain it was possible to pour into a single inhale. Then she added, "He is the Son of Heaven. He will know your virtue, and he will select you."

Ling Xin kept quiet, already familiar with the hard wall of her mother's prudishness. But she had to know, and her mother was the only person she could ask.

"Very well," she said, doing her best to appear meek. "Tell me about when you and father met. How is it that he chose you. Were you in love?"

"Love?" her mother scoffed. "That is something for fairy tales. You know better than to look for that."

She did. After all, hadn't that been Li Fei's downfall? "I am not looking for love. I want to know why father selected you. What did you do to make him choose you?"

Her mother folded her hands and frowned. "We met only once, you know, though he spoke to your grandfather many times." She grinned in memory. "Your grandmother and I watched through the screen. He was so handsome! He'd already passed the civil service exam. He was already an important person with a bright future in front of him. And look, now he is one of the emperor's closest advisors."

Ling Xin was very proud of her father. Less than one soul in a hundred passed the exam. And fewer than that rose high enough to advise the emperor. She smiled thinking of Zhi Hao. She hoped he would be as fortunate.

"So he spoke with grandfather before ever meeting you," Ling Xin prompted.

"Several times."

Which meant they'd married for one reason. "He wanted your dowry and grandfather's connections." Her grandfather had not passed the imperial exam. Indeed, it was one of the great failings in his life. But he had found his own way in making medicines. It was the basis of the family wealth.

But her mother did not like that characterization. "He would not have married me if I wasn't acceptable in every way," she said, her tone sharp.

"Of course, you are perfect."

The lady sniffed and returned to the pile of linens.

"But…" Ling Xin began.

"Oh, you do plague me," her mother complained. "What is it?"

"Mama," she said, abandoning her formal tone. "Every girl set before the emperor will be virtuous. He has no need of family connections nor my dowry. How can I become empress—or even a favored concubine—if I do not please him in other ways. In *physical* ways?"

Her mother blinked at her, her mouth agape. Then she abruptly frowned. "You are not to know those things!"

Ling Xin threw up her hands. "I will need them on my wedding night!"

"The eunuchs will teach you. And if not, then I will see you before the wedding. The girl's parents are allowed—"

"Not for the concubines. You will not see me if I am not

selected as empress. And you know there are other families with connections just as valuable as ours. We bring the emperor doctors and apothecaries."

"And bankers!"

Yes, her father had connections to money people throughout China. "Bankers are very important," Ling Xin agreed. "But there are others who bring control over land or alliances with other countries." She leaned forward. "Mama, I am one of many good candidates for empress. I am looking for a way to be even more attractive to the Son of Heaven so as to stand above everyone."

Her mother bit her lip. She knew it was true. And a moment later, Ling Xin knew that she had gotten through to her mother. The lady sagged in her seat and stared at her hands. Once she spoke, her words were so quiet that Ling Xin had to strain to hear.

"There is a book," she finally said. "Given to girls before their wedding night."

Ling Xin brightened. "Do you have it?"

Mama shook her head. "I was not given one, but your grandmother had one. I saw it when I was a child."

"What became of it?"

Her mother shrugged. "I will see if it is in her old things."

Ling Xin immediately hopped to her feet. "I can look—"

"You will practice your singing," Mama said sharply before slowly rising to her feet. "I will find it for you. If I cannot, perhaps I will ask your uncle. He will know how to get one."

It was the best she could hope for. But even so, it was a faint hope. Seduction required skill. Could she learn that from a book?

"Please find it soon, Mama. I need to learn it—"

Her mother pointed a single finger at her. The nail was sharp and very direct. "You will not open it until you have been selected. Only after you have been confirmed as a concubine may you know such things."

"Of course, Mama," Ling Xin said, keeping her voice low and her eyes downcast. She had to in order to get the book. But she knew it was a lie. She would open the thing the first private moment she had. She did not like being ignorant, and she would not go into her Feast of Fertility unprepared.

But the chances of her mother finding that book were slim. Which meant that there was only one path open to her now. And that path led to the garden wall after everyone else was abed.

CHAPTER SEVEN

"WHERE IS YOUR mind?"

Zhi Hao started at the sharp words from his tutor, but he was too slow to avoid the slap to the back of his head. It wasn't painful, but it was powerful enough to make his head jerk.

"Master Gao," he said, fighting to keep his tone respectful. "I am right here."

"Your ass is here." The man pointed to emphasize his crude words. "Your eyes are in the garden. I want to know where your mind is."

"On the meaning of—"

"Do not lie to me." The man's tone indicated that he would tolerate no more evasion.

Zhi Hao grimaced and looked down. He'd been terribly distracted today, and there was no hiding it. So he relented with as much grace as he could master.

"Please tell me about the Song daughter next door."

Master Hao's face softened. "Ah. You have heard her singing, haven't you?"

"Um—"

"She's quite talented, but that is not the Song daughter. That is the cousin, come to stay for a while with them."

Zhi Hao nodded, wondering just how much he should reveal of what had happened last night. Nothing, of course. But he wanted to know more about Ling Xin.

"What do you know of the Song daughter?" he pressed. "Not the cousin."

"Why?"

"Her family is powerful, yes? Her father—"

"He's an earl who advises the emperor on matters of finance. He has two sons, both smart, and yet neither passed the exam. And do you know why?"

Zhi Hao shook his head.

"Because they became distracted! Because they met women and thought of flower petals and creamy skin when they should…be….studying!" His last words were punctuated with stabs on the scrolls in front of Zhi Hao.

"Yes, master," Zhi Hao intoned. But though his head was bowed, his mind was racing. If the two sons of an earl could not pass the exam, what chance did he have? "Didn't their father pay the bribes?"

"Bribes? Don't be ridiculous! Imagine an earl attempting to cheat the exam. Everyone involved would be beheaded." He glared straight at Zhi Hao. "No man can pass the exam by bribery."

"Yes, Master Gao."

"Many have tried, to their shame. And punishment!"

"Yes, Master Gao."

"Do not think of trying to bribe anyone!"

Zhi Hao stifled his snort. He had no coin to bribe anyone. His only hope was to impress with his intelligence and knowledge of imperial policy, Confucian doctrine, and…and…

Damnation, he was tired. After last night's experience, he had been too filled with desire to sleep. The girl had been everything he wanted in a woman. Beautiful, refined, and with a sense of daring that made his cock twitch even now.

"Where is your mind?" Master Gao bellowed again, and Zhi Hao jolted, not at the sound but at the fact that his mind had wandered again. Why couldn't he focus?

He gripped his ink brush and let the words out despite Master Gao's irritation. "The Song daughter will have a large dowry, will she not?"

Master Gao grunted as he took a seat across from Zhi Hao. "So you are thinking of your future after you fail the exam. Already you have given up—"

"No!" Zhi Hao exclaimed. "*After* I pass the exam, my future will be assured. I will have status and an appointment."

"Depending on how high your score, yes. But appointments can take more than a year to come." Master Gao shook his head. "China's bureaucracy is as large as China itself."

It was an exaggeration, obviously, but not a large one.

"Still, my future will be assured," Zhi Hao repeated. "And once I pass, I will be an excellent choice as a bridegroom."

"And you think to marry the Song girl?" Laughter tore through Master Gao hard enough that he grabbed his belly. "You, with no family claim to greatness and only a eunuch uncle who begged me to help you. The earl will have a thousand suitors better than you."

"Not if I pass the exam!"

Master Gao grunted rather than agreed. Then he stared hard at his student, his brow furrowing as he let his hand bang down hard on the desk. "Perhaps you should apply yourself to passing the exam before you start thinking of girls."

Zhi Hao knew his teacher was right. He could not allow himself to be distracted. And yet his gaze kept returning to the garden and his mind kept thinking—

Master Gao's curse blistered the air. "Zhi Hao, what has happened? You were not this way before. You were diligent and attentive. Suddenly you cannot put two words down without making a mess of it."

Zhi Hao looked at the smeared characters on his paper. Master Gao was right.

"Did something happen?" the man asked. "Last night, what changed?"

"Nothing," Zhi Hao said. "I am merely thinking of—"

"Flower petals and creamy skin."

Well, yes.

"And the Song girl."

Zhi Hao swallowed. He had to give the master something or the man would never leave this topic. "I had a dream last night," he finally said. "It was of her and me. Of us married and—"

"A dream," the master said, leaning forward with a sharp movement. "What kind of dream?"

Zhi Hao shot his teacher a glare. He knew what kind of dream. Every boy past the age of eleven knew.

"I see," the man said, his words slowing as he clearly thought deeply about something. "Have you ever seen this dream woman before?"

"What? No."

"And how do you know it was the Song girl? Have you ever met her?"

"You know I have not," he lied again. Then he frowned. "She said—"

Again a curse blistered the air. "Think, boy!" the Master said with another heavy thunk of his fist on the desk. "Think logically about this dream."

"It was just a dream," Zhi Hao lied.

"You are not a man who stares out the window because of a dream."

No, he wasn't. He was a man who had experienced something incredible last night.

"And in this dream," the master pressed. "Did you release your seed?"

Zhi Hao refused to answer, but the heat in his cheeks likely told the tale.

But the master would not let him evade the question. "Answer me! Did you expend your chi? Your life force releases with your cum. So says the Yellow Emperor. Did you—"

"Yes!" Zhi Hao bit out. "Yes, I did." And it had been wonderful.

The man leaned back in his chair and regarded Zhi Hao. "And now you are tired, irritable, and unable to focus." The master shook his head. "Do you not see what has happened?"

Zhi Hao frowned. "Nothing has happened. I had a dream—"

"You were visited by a fox spirit, you idiot. A fox sent to distract you from passing the imperial exam. A fox spirit sent to drain you of your power. A fox spirit who will destroy you." Each sentence took on greater power as he spoke, and yet the message did not penetrate Zhi Hao's brain.

All he could say was, "A what?"

"Do you not have fairy tales in the south? Do you know nothing of the spirits—"

"Spirits?" Zhi Hao gaped. "Fairy tales? Master Gao, are you ill?"

The man grunted as he stood up and paced away. "You think the old tales are falsehoods."

"Superstition."

"Idiot tales for idiot women."

Zhi Hao set aside his brush and faced his master squarely. "Yes."

"You are wrong." The master crossed to a nearby table and poured himself a healthy measure of rice wine. "Did I not teach you that a ruler uses logic, but the people—"

"Are swayed by emotions. Yes."

Master Gao nodded. "By fantasies and tales."

Zhi Hao frowned as he tried to recall the exact text. He couldn't. That sounded close enough.

His master leaned back against the wall, regarding him with steady eyes. "So many people believe...because sometimes, the tales are real."

Zhi Hao gaped at the man. He could not believe what he was hearing. But before he could frame a response, the man held up his hand.

"In this, I will teach you the truth, but you will not repeat it to anyone. You will not say it on the exam. And if you ever become magistrate of a back woods, miserable county, you will know that out there, the spirits are real."

"But not in Peking?"

"Not that we admit out loud." Master Gao's eyes grew distant. "But the fox spirit is real. And she visits many young men of promise." He leaned forward, his eyes bright. "She takes their minds and their chi away." He abruptly thumped the side of Zhi Hao's head. "You are tired. You are distracted. You have been visited by that evil spirit." He slammed back the last of his wine. "The fox demons only come for those with a bright future. That is what they steal when they take your chi." He shook his head. "I never would have thought you were special. You come from the provinces. You have artists for parents. You are not one to lead our country."

"And yet you took our money anyway."

"Of course I did. You have to learn, don't you? I have to eat, don't I?"

"But you think I have no chance."

Master Gao made a non-committal response. A sound that showed indifference and surprise together.

"The fox spirit has visited you." He snorted. "That means you have a future to steal, assuming you have not already given it up." Then his gaze fixed hard on Zhi Hao. "If she comes to you again, you must resist! When she appears, tell her to be gone. And for heaven's sake, keep your seed to yourself!"

Zhi Hao had no response to this. Of course, he had heard of the mischievous fox spirit. His master had mentioned her when Zhi Hao had first come to live with him. But he'd forgotten about her. It was all superstition. According to myth, the fox spirit was a shapeshifting sprite who fooled evil men and teased tiny children. Sometimes she stole chi from the powerful to survive. Sometimes she lured unwary men to their doom. The tales were everywhere. But there was no truth in them…was there?

What was more probable? That a sheltered aristocratic woman had come to him last night, stroking him to orgasm? Or that a spirit had tempted him away from his path?

When he thought logically, he had to believe the fox spirit was more likely. And that set him back on his heels.

"You think she will come again?"

"She will continue to take your chi until you die. That is how she survives."

"And how do I best her?"

Master Gao grabbed the wine bottle again and waved it directly at Zhi Hao. "You tell her to leave! Banish the supernatural. You study as if your life depends on passing the exam. *Because it does!*"

Zhi Hao let his chin drop as he gazed at the text in front of him. "I will apply myself," he said firmly.

"Good."

"But if she is a fox woman, then I cannot simply send her away. She will return again and again."

Master Gao shook his head. "Arrogance! You cannot best a spirit. Her weakness is that she cannot take you unwillingly. Now that you know, you can defend yourself. But only if you send her away."

"But what about what she has already taken? How do I get my chi back?"

"The same way she took it from you. She must release into your hands, you must absorb the power she gives out." The master shook his head. "Do not think you can do this. Demons are clever. She will not give up more than she takes."

"I must make her come? That will give me her chi?"

Master Gao grunted his assent, but a moment later, he waved the whole discussion away.

"Do not try it, Zhi Hao. Your future is in passing the exam. So what say you? Do you study? Do you take the destiny that fortune is offering you?"

That answer was obvious. "Yes, Master Gao!"

"And when the fox returns, what will you do?"

"I will not give her what she wants."

The man poured himself the last drops of the rice wine. "Excellent."

He now knew what he had to do. He would take from her instead. She would release her chi into him.

Zhi Hao did not say those words out loud. His master would loudly berate him for his arrogance, but he knew he could do it. He knew he could touch her and bring out her life force, right into his hand. And then he would use her power to pass the exam.

But first he had to study. And then after dinner, he would make plans for when the fox returned.

CHAPTER EIGHT

L ing Xin couldn't have slept if she tried. Fortunately, she wasn't trying. She was waiting until everyone was abed to sneak out to her wall perch. But while she waited in the dark, her heart pounding, her mind spun with the possibilities of her choices.

She could rely on the emperor's perception of her virtue and wait to be selected.

Absolutely not. For one thing, what she'd already done with Zhi Hao had tainted her virtue. Besides, waiting passively for heaven to bestow a gift had never been her style.

Alternately, she could wait for her mother to find the book. She knew Mama had called for grandmother's stored trunks, but she had no idea if or when her mother would come across the mysterious book.

And again, that required passive waiting.

Which left her with her last option—she must learn everything she could from Zhi Hao without risking her virginity. That was something she could not lose. She would be checked in the Forbidden City, and if she did not pass the test of virginity, she would be thrown onto the street as trash.

Her father would not accept her back then. Not if she failed the virginity test. He had already told her that when she had her first menstrual period. That meant she would have to live with her aunt and uncle in the north, but what kind of life would she have there? Her uncle had already thrown away Li Fei and killed her lover. Li Fei was his daughter. How much worse would he treat his niece?

With her choice made, Ling Xin snuck outside and quietly climbed up to her perch on the wall. She noted with pleasure that yesterday's rain had brought more leaves onto the branches. With the moonlight beginning to wane, this was a very secluded bower.

At least, that was what she told herself, since stroking a man's dragon on a rock wall was not the sort of risk even a daring girl would take. Unless, of course, she was very desperate to learn.

As expected, she found Zhi Hao in Master Gao's garden. He wore no shirt, no shoes, and the moonlight played delightfully with his muscles as he worked through his exercises. She could see that he wasn't working very hard, and that he turned to look at her the moment she settled on the wall. Then before she could do more than smile, he bounded up beside her on the wall, perching like a bird in front of her.

"Good evening, Ling Xin," he said, his voice a throaty purr.

She shivered at the tone even as she sensed a note of hardness in it.

"Good evening, Zhi Hao," she whispered, her sense of danger climbing. "You seem different tonight."

"Me? No. Have you come for another lesson?"

She nodded slowly, concerned by the glittering anger she felt radiating from him. It was not right, and she instinctively shrank back from him.

"I do not think this is a good night to converse," she said. But as she turned to leave, his hand shot out and gripped her shoulder. Not hard enough to bruise, but strong enough to concern her.

"Tell me about yourself, Song Ling Xin," he said, a seductive note in his voice that worried her, even as it thrilled her. "Tell me about your family. What does your father do for the emperor?

What are your favorite fairy tales?"

What an odd set of questions. "Why?"

He smiled, the white of his teeth flashing bright in the moonlight. "So I know that you are real, Song Ling Xin. Tell me something that a spirit would not know."

She gaped at him. "You think me a spirit?"

"I think that the Song daughter would not be someone who climbs walls."

She almost laughed at that. "Then you don't know her very well, do you? I have been the bane of my nurse's existence since the day I was born. Hard on the breast as I sucked with all my might. Then running, always running, when I was little. My mother used to rub her temples as I rushed up and down the stairs out of boredom. I even did it in summer. No matter how hot it was, I could not sit still or I would scream. My mother used to wish that they had bound my feet so that I would cease moving."

He glanced down at her legs, hidden beneath her light robe. "Why aren't your feet bound?"

Did he know nothing? "Because it has been banned and no daughter of an earl would be so treated." She arched a brow. "How do you not know that?"

"I do know it. And yet, where I grew up, many girls are still crippled."

She grimaced. She had seen older women hobbling on their heels, growing fat because they tried to eat away their pain. She was fortunate to have been born of a Manchu bannerman. The Manchu had never bound their daughters' feet. That had been a custom of the conquered Han. And yet, all became China and some customs remained.

"My feet are strong," she said. "But my spirit..." She sighed. "My spirit has always been a little wild. Sometimes I think they bound women's feet because only then would they be content to live inside walls." She glanced out toward the street. How many times had she wanted to leap over the stone and run free? Nearly every day of her life. But she knew the cost. After all, Li Fei had been banished for wandering into the market and kissing a man.

Meanwhile, Zhi Hao was watching her. Did he see the shifting thoughts on her face? She couldn't tell, but in a moment, his expression softened and he gently stroked the back of her hand.

"The Forbidden City will be equally constricting," he said. "Once there, you will never leave."

She knew it was true. "At least it will be a bigger cage."

He exhaled with clear exasperation. "But you have options besides the Forbidden City. You would have more freedom if you married. If your husband was generous."

"And whom would I marry?" she countered in a whisper. "The butcher's son? The apothecary's nephew? You?"

His shoulders squared at the offense. "Would that be a bad life?"

Maybe not. But as the daughter of an earl in the year of the Festival of Fertility, her path was set. "My father has declared that I will be empress."

"He has high aim."

Of course he did. No man became counsel to the emperor without it. "He says it must be. He said I must make it so. He has said that since the moment I was born a girl."

"But how?" he pressed.

That was the very question she had been asking all day. All week. Perhaps all her life.

"I am here so you may teach me," she stressed. Then she reached for the ties of his pants.

He caught her well before she could touch him. "You have seen my dragon. You have seen how it releases. But that is like seeing the end of a story without learning about the beginning."

She lifted her gaze to his. "How do I begin?"

"You must show the emperor, from the first moment he sees you, that you are excited to be with him."

She shrugged. "I will be excited. Everyone will be."

"Not excited in that way. You must be aroused, so to make

him equally aroused."

She had no idea what he meant. She could not even begin to ask.

He shook his head. "You do not know any of this, do you? Have you even thought of men and what happens in the bedroom?"

She bristled at the implied lack. She was not a woman who lacked for anything. But the moment her pride surged hot, logic held it back. What she lacked was knowledge, and that was the exact reason she was here.

"I thought of you last night," she said. "And the emperor always."

He leaned forward before she could frame an answer about the bedroom. "I know you had not kissed a man before. Did you like it?"

She'd liked it so much that she wanted to kiss him again. She wanted to feel all of his muscles touching her body once more. All that power surrounding her again.

The idea was thrilling.

"I have seen lovers," she finally said. "From the other place on the wall where I first saw you. Sometimes I sit there and watch the street. And sometimes late at night, I see things."

"Couples in an embrace?"

"Yes." She smiled and felt her lips tingle. Now she knew what that felt like. Now she knew the tangle of tongues, the rapid beat of her heart, and the liquid heat down low in her belly.

"Ah," he said, his tone back to that throaty purr. "You are thinking about it. You are remembering last night?" There was a satisfied note in his words.

She ignored it. Let him think that he was an amazingly skilled lover. He was probably terrible. It was only that she had no way of knowing any different. Meanwhile, she had to keep to her purpose.

"You are saying that I should remember our kiss. When I meet the emperor, I should think on that?"

"Angel, that is only the beginning of what you must remember. You must know it all."

"All?" That sounded dangerous.

"Arousal, Ling Xin. From the beginning to the sweet end."

She shook her head. That made no sense. "How can there be an end?"

He dropped back onto his haunches. "Think, Ling Xin. If you are who you say you are, then apply your mind to the act. You saw my release last night. Tonight, you must experience your own."

She pulled back, alarmed. "I will not lose my virginity to you!"

He held out a hand as if to stop her, but it was his chuckle that froze her in place. "I will not touch your virginity, I swear. But this is the next lesson. And to experience it, you must surrender to me."

"No." She was not about to surrender to anyone.

"Come into my bedroom, Ling Xin. Master Gao snores, so we will know when he wakes. I will not take anything from you save what is given in release."

Now she swung her legs over to her side of the wall, preparing to leave. He was clearly a cad who wanted the same thing all men wanted. "Do you take me for an idiot? I will not go into your bedroom!"

He shrugged. "Then experience it here, as I did last night." His eyes were serious. "I meant to make it more comfortable for you, that is all."

She did not trust him. She should run away. But before she leaped down, she remembered just what was at stake. She had no other option. He was the only one who could teach her. What if he was right? What if this was the next step?

She didn't know, and she silently damned her parents for not giving her the information she needed. How could they expect her to win over the emperor without giving her the training she needed to do it?

He clearly saw her indecision. And as she hesitated, he pointed to a perch in the tree. "I will make it safe for you. I will lean back there. You will sit between my legs."

"Between your legs! But—"

"With your back to my front. I cannot take your virginity from there. You know the basics. You know it is not possible."

She frowned, trying to see what he suggested. She supposed it looked sturdy enough. "But there is not room for me to…" She bit her lip, unwilling to finish her sentence.

He arched his brows as her words trailed away. "Angel, I must know what you are thinking. I cannot teach you without knowing what you do not understand."

She grimaced, seeing his logic but hating to voice the words. Nevertheless, she forced them out. "I will not be able to kiss you. How will I stroke your dragon—"

He smiled, his teeth glittering in the moonlight. "You will not touch my dragon except with your back. I will not release my seed tonight. But you, you must feel everything. You will give up your chi to me. If you want to catch an emperor, that is."

His words rang with challenge, but she didn't understand it. Of course she wanted to catch the emperor. Hadn't she said so? And how was her chi involved? He made no sense.

"Come now," he said. "Where is the Ling Xin who was bold enough to squeeze me so perfectly?"

"I am right here," she snapped. "But this is—"

"Dangerous? Every part of this play is."

She knew that. To rest there between his thighs, to allow him to surround her like that…

It shamed her to think how much she wanted that. How desperately she tingled at the thought. But…

"I will be vulnerable," she finally said. "To whatever you want to do. I do not know you well enough for that."

He nodded as if that made sense, but he had a logical response. "You will be no more vulnerable than I was last night. Besides, you can protect yourself well enough. I will show you how."

He maneuvered around her, shifting on the wall to climb into the branches. And as he moved, she smelled his scent, heard his breath, and even felt the ripple of his muscles as he adjusted around her.

She shifted away quickly. She had to, or she'd have fallen off the stone wall. But the more time he took maneuvering, the more she allowed herself to "accidentally" feel him, "inadvertently" push against him, and of course, "ignorantly" linger close.

She was a fool. She knew it. She felt the lure of him every second she was in his presence. She felt the burn of desire and knew her judgement was suspect. But she could not stop herself. She wanted to experience what he was offering.

"See?" he said as he finally settled. "If you slam your head back against my chest, I will fall back. This is safe for some things, but not if you object." He glanced down into his courtyard. "It will be a bad fall for me if you fight."

She saw what he meant. His legs were braced, one on a branch, one hanging over the side. If she was between his thighs, a hard shove backwards could push him over. Indeed, a well-placed elbow might even do it.

"You are safe," he said.

Not exactly. She quickly saw why he was suggesting this position. If she sat between his thighs, he would be able to touch all of her. His hands could move freely over her body. And she would not be able to do anything but lean back and experience whatever he wanted her to feel.

"Where will I set my hands?"

"Wherever you like. But perhaps hold on here." He rustled a nearby branch, one that was sturdy enough to steady her. It might even be strong enough for her to swing into her garden if he did something she didn't like.

Oh, how tempted she was!

They looked at one another as she struggled with indecision. He didn't force her. Indeed, he said nothing. He simply sat with his arms spread, waiting for her to decide.

"What will you do?" she finally asked.

"I will kiss your neck," he said. "And I will stroke your breasts."

At his words, she felt her skin prickle as if he were already doing as he said.

"And then…" His voice trailed away.

"What?"

"I will raise your skirt and use my fingers, pretending it is my dragon."

Her belly clenched at that. Not in fear, but in desire.

"You must know what it feels like without losing your virginity. You must experience what it is to be taken by the emperor so he will lose his seed inside you."

"But—"

"It is only pretend, Ling Xin. You will pass the virginity exam."

She nodded because she wanted to believe him.

"I will feel it all?" she asked, her voice a whisper of need.

"I swear it." He grinned at her. "It is the only way to know. You must—"

"Yes." The word escaped before she could stop herself.

She carefully turned around on the wall, settling herself gingerly between his thighs. And when she struggled with her legs dangling on opposite sides of the wall, he guided her to put one leg over his where he braced himself on the branch. And the other…

Oh my. The other went across his dangling one, leaving her legs spread wide, her skirt tight across her thighs, and…

And his hands tightened across her belly. Her breath caught. His hands were so large, so warm. And then he began to kiss her neck. Heat and pressure. A sweet lick that made her body tighten with desire.

So fast. So open! And yet as his tongue slid across her damp skin, she shivered in delight. This felt nice. With his teeth scraping across her flesh, she felt tingly.

Her belly fluttered. Her body felt surrounded and so safe that she relaxed further against him.

"Remember," he murmured against her ear. "If you are afraid, you can slam your head backwards against me. You might even knock me unconscious."

She twisted to see behind him. Yes, he was not perched so solidly that she couldn't throw him off.

"You have control," he said.

She nodded slowly, saying the words aloud in order to convince herself.

"I have control," she said hoping it was true.

He waited as she turned to face forward again, with him at her back. She felt his hands slip around her waist and she shivered at the sweet feel. It was especially thrilling because his hands were not still. Indeed, her belly tingled as his hands slipped slowly, inevitably up from her waist.

Inch by inch, his hands crept higher while she held her breath in anticipation. And then, he cupped her. On both sides, he held her breasts in his two hands.

That was when she realized she had no control at all.

CHAPTER NINE

L ING XIN FELT it all. Her mind grasped and held on to every sensation, every detail, memorizing it, in the way that only the most diligent student could. Or at least she tried to, because to admit that she relished every second, was thrilled to the core with every caress, would be to admit that she wanted to be debauched in the most carnal way.

She wanted what he was doing, and so she gave herself up to the experience of it all.

His hands were on top of her night dress. The thin silk, however, did nothing to blunt the feel of his large hands gently cupping her breasts. She arched in reaction, simultaneously trying to move away and lifting herself deeper into his hands.

It made no sense. Oh heaven, her heart was racing so fast, and he was doing nothing but holding her.

His breath heated her ear, his tongue teasing across the shell. She shivered in reaction and her toes curled inside her slippers.

"Tell me what you feel," he whispered.

"Everything," she confessed.

"You must know the details specifically. You must remember what makes you feel good, what is too much, and what is exquisite."

Such words! Did she feel exquisite? Her body was shifting, moving of its own volition. And yet, she could not stop.

His palms pressed into her breasts, and then his fingers began to move. She felt them roll over her nipples, and the peaks tightened unbearably.

"Too much!" she gasped.

He immediately eased his grip, softening his hands until her breasts lay gently in his palms. And still his fingers moved over her nipples, the edge of his thumbnail tweaking the peaks.

"Better?" he asked, and she heard a note of humor in his tone.

"Are you laughing at me?" she asked. She knew the tone of a man mocking a woman. His was not quite there, but—

"I mock myself, angel. Your breasts are sublime. Feel how I react to them." So saying, he thrust his hips forward slightly. She felt the press of his dragon, hot and hard against her back.

It aroused him to touch her? She supposed that made sense. The making of children was supposed to be a mutual thing, was it not? Enjoyable to both?

To test this, she rolled her back against his dragon, flowing her spine along his ridge, and then grinned when she heard him hiss in reaction.

"You liked that?' she asked.

In answer, he pinched her nipples. The pain was sharp and sweet all at once. Her gasp was both one of surprise and delight.

"You liked that?" he asked, and this time she knew he teased her.

But she was too far gone to care what either of them felt so long as it was more. More excitement, more tingling, more need as she dropped her head back against his broad shoulder and lifted her chest.

"Do it again," she said. "And I will do it back."

"Fox," he said, his voice low, "you torture me."

She smiled. She liked that she had some power here. "Shall I turn around?"

"No." His voice was firm as were his hands where they pressed against her breasts. No longer teasing, he was holding her in place.

"But—"

"Hush. You have not reached completion yet. We cannot stop until you do."

She didn't know what that meant, but she trusted him. Indeed, she very much feared she would let him do anything as long as he kept teasing her breasts the way he was. His strokes were varied and delightful, as if he was totally caught up in playing with her body, seeing when she gasped, what made her arch, and what made her sigh in delight.

He squeezed her breasts, pulled at the nipples, and moved them how he willed. And all the time, he whispered words that made her throat go dry. For all that she saw him as a fighter, nightly destroying phantom enemies in his practice, he was also a scholar. Words were his true weapons, and he used them to great effect now.

"Men love breasts," he said as his breath coiled about her ear. "We love to hold them, to touch them. We like to suck them and imagine our organ surrounded by them."

They were strange words to her ears, but when he matched them with his actions, she felt the truth of it in her body. Especially when his fingers pulled at her nipples as if he were suckling them right now. Every pull had her belly tightening. Every pinch made her back arch as if seeking more. She was so absorbed in what he did that she barely noticed when he raised his knees and pulled them wide. And as he widened his knees, her legs spread even more open.

She loved the breeze as it cooled her most intimate petals. And when the heat there built unbearably, she welcomed the way he pulled her gown up until she was exposed to the full night sky.

If she'd had the breath to speak, she might have objected. Indeed, she could have fought him if she wanted.

She did not.

She wanted his hands to flow across her belly. And when his two hands left her breasts to squeeze her thighs, she reveled in their strength…and held her breath in anticipation.

"Do you feel wet? Do you smell your scent?"

Yes and no. The air was redolent with both of their scents, both of their heat. Behind her back, she felt his dragon pulse. Between her thighs, his fingers moved across her thighs. They inched into the crease between thigh and mons.

Then he wiggled his fingers.

Her entire body pulsed. Her thighs quivered and yet he had done nothing but touch her legs. She wanted his fingers closer. She felt the breeze tease her heated flesh. And when he did not move, she whimpered.

"Are you ready?" he murmured against her cheek. "This is your first time. It may go fast."

Every part of her was ready, but she knew better than to beg. Instead, she rolled her spine against him and grinned when he gasped.

"Very well, Fox," he said. And then he slowly pressed his fingers down. She was so wet, they moved easily, slipping across bone and down into her petals.

She gasped as his hands opened her wider, slipping the thickness of his fingers everywhere. And yet, it was not what she wanted. She didn't understand. She could only feel.

"I love your scent," he said as he scooped up some of her moisture and brought it to her nose. It was a strange smell, but erotic enough that she inhaled deeply. "And I love the taste," he continued as he licked his fingers.

What a sight! His dark tongue lapping around his wet finger.

"It's a woman's chi," he continued. "The essence of creation." He pressed a kiss to her temple. "We drink it and grow strong."

She frowned, the meaning in his words triggering a memory. Her brother had studied secret texts, ones which were forbidden for her to read. But that hadn't stopped her. She had devoured them in secret, including the words of the Yellow Emperor about life essence and…

And this! This churning of desire was life force! When he touched her, when he heated the cauldron in her belly, he was bringing forth her energy. This was womanly essence, and now she knew why men sought it and why women allowed it. It was for this feeling, for this stirring of everything that was female.

And now she understood why the Yellow Emperor had said that drinking of a woman gave man life. And that releasing of a man's seed wasted his chi.

Is that what he was doing? Every time he swept up her moisture, every time he wrapped his tongue around his fingers, was he drinking in her energy? She had barely thought the questions through when he answered them.

"Here is the cauldron of female power," he said as he began to stroke her petals. "Do you feel it churn?"

She felt her belly quivering, her bottom lifting and lowering as she sought his fingers. Behind her back, she felt his dragon pulse, but it was only one of a thousand sensations overwhelming her. His one hand held her thigh open while the other pushed a finger inside her.

She felt the callouses of his palms, the invasion as he wriggled inside, and she found it all fascinating. He pressed in and out with a single finger. And then…

She gasped.

Two fingers, stretching her open. She closed her eyes. It felt so good.

"My dragon will go there," he said. "It will burrow deep."

His fingers moved inside her, and she groaned in delight. Still, she had the wherewithal to shake her head.

"Not you. It is for the emperor." The words were rote, a mantra she had been told since she was a child. Her glory was meant for the ruler of China.

Zhi Hao grunted as if annoyed. "Do not speak of another man when one is inside you," he growled.

With that, he thrust a third finger inside her, stretching her in a way that made her feel impaled and opened all at once. How could something so invasive feel so good? Her legs widened as he thrust his fingers in and out.

"Your channel is tight. I like that," he said. Then he set his teeth on her neck, abrading her hard enough to make her feel pinned above and below.

"This is what a man will do. He will thrust in you as you grip him." He tongued the skin where he had bit her. "Do it, Fox. Squeeze my fingers, and I will give you what you want."

She wasn't sure how to do it, but her body did. As he thrust up inside her, she squeezed him until he groaned. And then his thumb moved upward.

Lightning shot through her.

She cried out at the shock of it, and he immediately bit down on her ear.

"Shhh! Keep your cries inside you. Can you be silent even as I do this? And this?"

He was thrusting inside her as his thumb pressed harder against her other spot.

"This is your pearl," he growled against her ear. "I will make it shine."

He did. He rubbed it once, then twice, while her body undulated in wild abandon. She did not know how he held her. She was moving, arching, needing.

Then he stopped. Everything stilled, trembling on the edge of madness.

"More?" he rasped.

In answer, she jerked backwards enough to hit hard against his dragon.

"More," she commanded.

"Yes," he agreed. Then she felt him thrusting against her back, his hips working his dragon along her spine as he thrust his fingers into her.

And that glorious pearl he polished? It ached for him. It ached, wanting him. Then he spread her thighs as wide as they would go, and he rubbed his calloused finger all the way up.

Her pearl vibrated, and her body echoed it.

"More," she gasped. "Please."

His growl was low and thrilling. "Ask me again," he said as he rubbed her faster. Harder.

She hadn't the breath.

So close!

"Please!"

Yes!

It was as if her body vibrated itself apart with bigger and bigger waves until she was soaring into pleasure. Such bliss! She felt suffused by it.

She heard him grunt behind her, felt the wetness of his release against her back, and she knew that men did indeed enjoy a woman's pleasure.

Or at least he had. And she was well pleased. Indeed, she didn't think she had ever been so pleased in her entire life.

She floated, alight and alive in his arms. She listened to his ragged breath as she drifted in sweetness.

"I want to do that every day and night," she murmured. "If I were allowed, I would never stop."

He didn't answer. Indeed, she began to wonder at his silence. Had she done something wrong?

She twisted her head to look at him. His face was in shadow, but she saw his expression. It was not quite angry. Not quite joyous. Rueful?

"Why do you frown?" she asked.

"Your body is beautiful," he finally rasped. "Your skin glows in moonlight and when you are flushed with passion, you seem to shimmer."

"It is the silk. There are gold threads in the design."

He shook his head. "It was you. Open. Glorious. How could I stop myself?"

"What?" she straightened, suddenly afraid. "What have you done?"

"Nothing to harm your virginity, Ling Xin. I did not mean to give you my chi this night." He gestured down at himself where his pants were wet with his release.

"But that is good, yes? That is what I want. To excite the emperor enough that—"

"Yes," he interrupted a bit harshly. "Yes, that is what you want. Heavenly nectar for China's great emperor." His tone was bitter, and she suddenly understood that he was jealous. Of course, he was. All men wanted to be the emperor.

"If I could choose," she said softly. "I would watch you from behind the women's screen when you spoke with my father. I would burn incense and pray that he chose you."

He sighed and touched her temple with his. "That is a lovely dream," he finally said. "But there is not enough time."

"For what?"

"For me to pass the imperial exam. For me to receive a place in government high enough that I can support myself and my sisters." He sighed. "To support a wife."

She understood what he was saying. What they were both saying. If things were different, he would court her in the usual way. He would apply to her father and perhaps she would be able to whisper her preference into her father's ear. But Zhi Hao needed something to show his value. Something like a good appointment with a good salary.

There was not enough time for him to do all that before the Feast of Fertility in a month. And even if there were time, her father would never allow her to have a husband who was not the emperor.

Zhi Hao looked at her, and then he slowly drew his wet fingers up to his mouth. He licked it, his eyes drifting shut as he did so. The sight was eerie, and yet so erotic that she felt her belly tighten again. And when he was done, he looked down at her.

"I have drunk so little of your chi, Fox," he murmured. "It is nothing compared to what you have taken from me."

"Taken?" she snorted. "I took nothing from you. And why do you call me a fox?" She twisted so that she could face him more squarely.

"Because I cannot believe you are the Song daughter spreading her thighs here for me. It is not possible."

"So you think me a fox spirit instead?"

"It is that or believe you are a flesh and blood woman that I can never have."

She shook her head. "You are an idiot." She twisted her legs together, thankful that the stone wall was very thick. It gave her room to maneuver. "And you will never pass the exam if you believe fox spirits haunt you."

With that, she walked away from him, looking for the chair she had set against the wall. There might be moonlight, but it was still dark here in this corner of the garden. Besides, her legs were heavy, her spirit languid. She had no understanding of the nonsense he was spouting. Did a man's release make him addlebrained?

He watched her in the darkness, the white of his eyes eerie in the moonlight. He neither moved to assist her nor straightened against the tree. He stared at her with a bemused expression half forlorn, half awed.

"Zhi Hao—" she began, but he cut her off.

"You shimmered at your completion."

"I am a normal woman. I am not a deity, even a small one."

"You are so much more than a normal woman," he said as he finally got up and walked over to her, holding out his hand to help her descend. "Even if you are not a fox, you are exquisite." His voice broke on the last word, as if it meant more to him than she knew.

"Good night, Zhi Hao," she said. "Thank you for teaching me this."

Then she dropped down to the ground. Thankfully, her legs held her up. Her footfalls might be a bit heavy, but she was strong enough to put the chair back where it belonged. And as she did, a flicker of movement caught her eye.

It was a shadow that flitted past her into the greenery. A hint of red, a flash of a bushy tail, and two eyes that blinked at her.

She gasped and spun around, but there was nothing there.

Nothing except her imagination. He had called her fox, and so she had made one out of the shadows. There was nothing there except darkness and the lingering bliss that still suffused her body.

Now she understood the Yellow Emperor's words about a woman's chi. Now she knew why men sought copulation so desperately. The feelings were amazing. And now she wondered...

How much more was there for her to know? If such bliss was part of life and she hadn't even guessed, what more did Zhi Hao know that she did not? And how could she get him to teach her everything?

CHAPTER TEN

Z HI HAO WAS fully dedicated to his studies. At least that's what he told himself. In truth, he spent much of his time trying to figure out if his nighttime visitor was flesh and blood or a fox spirit sent to steal his life force. The question was driving him crazy, making him question his own sanity.

Ling Xin felt like a true flesh and blood woman to him, one who set his body on fire. And yet, no daughter destined for the Feast of Fertility would do the things she did.

She must be a vixen. And yet the very idea was ridiculous.

Either way, Master Gao had tripled his efforts to be sure Zhi Hao was ready for the exam. It would have been hard for him to manage the tasks set before him even if he hadn't spent the night dreaming of the fox woman.

Never before had he experienced anything so magical. He knew it was nothing more than physical arousal, and yet he already knew so much more about her now, things that attracted him even more than her body. She was daring and smart. At the beginning, they'd spent a great deal of time debating philosophies and he'd found her mind as agile as his own. That was rare in a man, and unheard of in a woman. And therein lay the question.

Could any woman be so perfect?

He had to know, and so he set about devising a way to meet the lady during the day. Normally, a wealthy daughter was kept away from all young men until it was time for her to wed. Unfortunately, Ling Xin was destined for the emperor, so he would not be able to meet her in the normal course of events.

But he still had a plan. It only needed Master Gao to agree to help him during tomorrow's Chingming festival.

"Master Gao, wouldn't it be smart for me to speak with someone who has passed the imperial exam? Just to get his advice."

His teacher looked up from where he'd been filling his pipe. "I have taken the exam. Why would you—"

"Of course, you understand a great deal. But what about Earl Song? Does he not live next door? Did you not teach his two sons?"

"Of course I did, but those lazy dullards didn't pass. They didn't apply themselves, and their father blames me. He is a fool!" And with that, Master Gao went back to his pipe, sucking on it with hard, angry breaths.

"I see. I see," Zhi Hao continued as if thinking deeply. "You know, I hear the ladies talking in the garden next door."

"You should not listen to all that silly chattering."

"But I hear that a cousin has come to visit. A woman named Li Fei."

Master Gao grunted. "So? You need to stop thinking of women."

"I was thinking of her younger brothers. Will they not need to be taught by someone?"

"I told you. Earl Song has no faith in me. I failed his sons. He thinks I will fail his nephews." He stood up and headed for the back garden. Zhi Hao had to catch him before he left completely.

"But if you flatter him," he pressed. "If you take me to learn from him—"

"Then he will believe me even more inept." The tone was mournful now rather than angry.

"Or he will recognize your intelligence. After all, flattery is always useful when used judiciously. And he knows a great deal about the emperor."

Master Gao turned to him. "Why do I need to know about the emperor?"

Wasn't that obvious? "To know what he wants in his officials. So that I can say it in my examination essays."

For all that Master Gao was irritable, he was no fool. He paused in the doorway as he puffed on his pipe.

"You make a compelling argument." Master Gao drew himself to his full height. "But you took much too long to think of it. I have been waiting for you to suggest such a thing." He folded his arms across his chest. "Now tell me how we can best achieve this feat?"

"Perhaps a dinner request?"

Master Gao snorted. "I cannot ask an earl to invite us to dinner. Think, boy!"

Zhi Hao was thinking. Indeed, he'd been chewing on this for the better part of the morning.

"Tomorrow is the Chingming Festival," he said. "I must honor my ancestors and give them a bounty so that I may pass the imperial exam, yes?"

"You can make your bows in the courtyard where you practice your exercises."

Zhi Hao nodded. "I could, but perhaps there is someone important that you should honor? Perhaps at the Song shrine?"

His master frowned. "Why would I honor…" His voice trailed away as he considered the possibility. "It would be an act of contrition for failing to teach his lazy sons. I could clean the family tomb." He narrowed his eyes as he looked at Zhi Hao. "*We* could scrub the dirt away and leave an offering. And if the earl finds the work acceptable, then we can give him our bows and he will be grateful."

"That's a great idea. You truly are a master," he said.

Sadly, the man was too smart to be fooled. "I am not as stupid as you think. And this could go very badly. But if you wish to take the chance of angering the earl, then we will attempt it."

Zhi Hao frowned. "Why would cleaning his tombs anger the Song patriarch?"

The man rolled his eyes. "Chingming is a holiday for a man to honor his ancestors. Do you think Earl Song has others do his duty for him?"

Zhi Hao didn't know. He knew very little about his neighbor. That was the whole point of this exercise: to learn more about the entire family.

"You know him best, Master Gao."

The man puffed more on his pipe before answering. "He will know that we are begging for favor."

"Everyone wants a favor, but we will earn it."

His master considered this. Eventually, he nodded. "We will clean most of the tomb, but not all. That will leave him a way to do his duty."

That was wise and Zhi Hao said so. He was grateful that Master Gao was keen on his plan, even though they both knew Zhi Hao would do all the cleaning.

It didn't matter. On this holiday, all families honored their ancestors. The entire household, including the women, would be there, showing their devotion. Indeed, if the Song daughter was vying to become empress, then she would likely be on her knees showing complete devotion.

All he needed to do was watch from the side. Then he would be able to tell if she was the woman who haunted his nights or a fox phantom.

That was his plan. But he needed to be clearheaded. So tonight, he would hoard his chi. He would not see her on the wall, though his body craved another rendezvous. He could not risk giving more of his life force to a spirit.

Not until he met the Song daughter for real and knew the truth of her.

CHAPTER ELEVEN

Ling Xin was overwhelmingly tired. The Chingming festival was tomorrow where she'd offer gifts to her ancestors in hopes of good fortune at the Feast of Fertility. To draw the most favor, she'd spent the day making festival cakes and folding joss paper into intricate offerings. Her hands and legs ached from the work, but it was necessary before she attempted anything so grand as becoming the Empress of China.

Either way, it was done now, and she had to fight sleep as she waited to see Zhi Hao. It was agonizing to wait, but she couldn't stop dreaming about the sensation of having his hands on her body. About the fire in her belly whenever he was near. And—strangely enough—she kept recalling the quiet way he'd held her when the bliss was over.

For all that the man fought invisible enemies when he exercised, she knew him to be a gentle man at heart. At least with her. And that made her body melt with desire. He made her feel safe. He would never hurt her, never destroy her chances, never take what she was unwilling to give.

Or so she believed… Finally, when it was dark enough, when she finally heard her family's snores as they slept, she crept out to her garden spot and climbed the wall to watch Zhi Hao exercising.

Except he wasn't there.

She leaned forward, scanning the shadows to see if he was somewhere else. She even walked the rock wall to see better, but he…

She spotted him. He was leaning against the back door, clearly waiting for her. But what was he doing there?

She leaned forward far enough that he could see her and she, him. She gestured with her hands for him to come closer because she wasn't going to his bed. Their time together would be on this wall or not at all.

Apparently, that meant not at all. Because after locking eyes with her, he pointedly turned his back to her and walked into the house. He left the garden door open, no doubt thinking she would change her mind.

She did not.

Some things she would not risk, and her virginity was at the top of the list.

Still, it was unbelievably difficult to leave the garden. She had been looking forward to their time together. Besides, she'd become used to spending time with him, even before he'd started to train her.

It didn't matter, she told herself as she stomped off to bed. She was tired anyway. And if he had no desire to teach her, she had no desire to learn from him. Unfortunately, her dreams were another matter. They filled her mind and body with such imaginings that she woke in a sweat. Such erotic dreams! And all featuring the man who had turned his back on her last night.

"Are you still asleep? Get up!" Li Fei hauled the covers back, and Ling Xin glared at her. "Don't look at me that way!" her cousin said, her hands dropping onto her hips. "The sun is already up. You haven't bathed, and we must leave to honor your ancestors before noon."

Ling Xin groaned as she sat up. Her entire body felt achy from a night spent dreaming of love play. Could muscles ache from such a thing?

"Ling Xin!" her cousin snapped.

"Why before noon?"

"Because your father fears assassins."

Now that had her attention. She turned to stare at her cousin. "Assassins? Truly?"

Li Fei tsked as she pulled Ling Xin out of bed. "He manages the empire's gold. Do you not think there are people who might be angry about that? About who gets the gold and who doesn't?"

"Of course there are," Ling Xin said. The poor were everywhere in the city. "But that is not father's fault. He spends the money according to the emperor's command." And he was doing his best to fight the corruption of the eunuchs who stole constantly from the coffers. Or so she had heard her father grumble more than once. "None of that is his fault."

"The poor don't know that." Li Fei shook her head. "What is wrong with you lately? You're so distracted, so unfocused." She started pulling off Ling Xin's night clothes. "You cannot meet the emperor in such a state. He will toss you aside for sure."

"Would that be so bad a fate?" she muttered under her breath. Unfortunately, Li Fei was close enough to hear.

"What has gotten into you?" she gaped.

"Have you heard what it is like in the Forbidden City?"

Her cousin snorted. "Yes, I have. There is always food and good clothing to wear. Servants help you with everything. The cares of the world do not enter there."

"Neither do other men. What if I end up in the lower harem? I will never see the emperor, never bear his child. I'll be surrounded by eunuchs for the rest of my life." She shuddered at the thought. "At least when you marry, you will have children and a full life."

"If not a full belly," Li Fei countered. "The Forbidden City does not sound so bad to me."

"Married on the outside does not sound so bad to me."

The two cousins stared at each other, both aching for the other's fate. If only they could choose for themselves, but they both knew that was not the way in China. Not for the daughters of high-ranking bannermen.

Eventually, Ling Xin took her wishful heart in hand and stuffed it away. She had to be on her best behavior when making her gifts to the ancestors. If she could not learn more from Zhi Hao, then at least she would be the best daughter possible. She would show her devotion to her ancestors, and they would bless her.

"Come on," she said as she tugged on her cousin's sleeve. "The water will be cold soon."

"The water is cold now," her cousin retorted, but the two rushed away.

Two hours later, the household was headed for the Song family tomb. Not just herself, but her parents, and Li Fei. Her father brought a few retainers along as well, older men good with a sword. Her brothers and their families would meet them there.

It was a good morning for a gathering, and Ling Xin relished the spring heat in the air. The world was coming alive, and she would soon as well, according to her father. She would be a spring bride for the emperor, even though the Feast of Fertility wasn't until summer.

Ling Xin didn't argue. She had on all her best clothing, cosmetics, and adornments. In truth, she felt like a weighted down doll, but she could wear no less when she presented her gifts to the ancestors. Worse, it was difficult to walk in her shoes and almost impossible to see through the curtain of jade beads set before her eyes that was part of her hair piece.

Still, she managed it, shuffling behind her mother to the Song tomb, until she heard gasps all around her. Not gasps of fear, but ones of surprise. She tilted her head to see better.

And then had to pull the curtain of jade away from her eyes just to be sure.

Zhi Hao stood beside the Song tomb, his head bowed respectfully. Master Gao was with him, but Ling Xin only had eyes for her nighttime tutor. He stood taller than his master, his muscles slightly obscured by his student robes. He'd clearly been working because she saw beads of sweat on his forehead, but that was the only indication of toil.

Except for the sparkling stone edifice, cleaned of dirt and debris. The family tomb looked spotless.

Zhi Hao had done it all, she was sure, though Master Gao appeared mussed as he made his bows to her father.

"Greetings, Earl Song. I have come to show my devotion to your family, honoring your ancestors even before my own."

At the front of their procession, her father grunted, though Ling Xin knew he wasn't angry. If anything, he was pleased by that act, though he would never admit it out loud. Sure enough, a moment later, she heard her father's gruff voice.

"And why would I ask you to do my duty?"

"You did not, honored earl. And I have left the place of honor for your honest toil."

At this, Zhi Hao stepped aside to show a small square in the very center of the edifice that was still marked by dirt. Bowing his head, he held out a coarse bristle brush to her father.

Her father took the implement, but he didn't kneel to work. Instead, he glared at Zhi Hao. "Who is this?" he demanded.

"My newest student, honored earl."

Zhi Hao gave his greeting, speaking his name in a strong voice.

"I am Ko Zhi Hao. It is a great honor to meet you, Earl Song. You are the first I have ever met who has passed the imperial exam."

Her father snorted. "And I am likely the last." He turned to Master Gao. "What say you, Master? Is he smarter than my sons?"

And here Master Gao had a problem, because her two brothers and their wives had arrived as well. They flanked her father on either side and would not appreciate being insulted in favor of a young student.

"Not smarter. Not by any measure."

"Then he has no hope—" her father said, but Master Gao hedged.

"But Ko Zhi Hao studies diligently. Indeed, I believe him to be especially favored."

"Really?" Doubt was heavy in her father's voice. "How so?"

"Because he and his mother—on the very same night—dreamed an angel showed them the star above his head."

That would not sway her father. Dreams meant nothing to him, those made at night or during the day. Fortunately, Master Gao did not pause to give her father time to comment.

"Dreams of a mother and a boy can be dismissed. I thought nothing of it myself until I saw the proof myself."

At this, everyone lifted their heads to hear better, Ling Xin included.

"What proof?" her father demanded.

"A fox spirit, honored earl. A fox spirit has tempted him twice now. It tries to steal his chi so that he will fail. But I have counseled him to refuse it, and he has *listened*." There was extra emphasis on that last word. Enough that it made her brothers shift where they stood. How many times had Master Gao complained that her brothers never paid attention to what he was telling them?

"A fox spirit?" her father scoffed. "You have seen it?"

"I have seen red fur and angry eyes. And I have seen its power over Ko Zhi Hao." His voice dropped a note. "He confessed to me that he released his chi to the demon."

Demon! Was that what he thought of her?

It was all Ling Xin could do to keep still. It was absolutely ridiculous for anyone to think she was the vixen who had seduced him. He was the one with all the knowledge. But as ridiculous as it sounded, her father seemed intrigued. He even tossed an arch look at his sons as he commented.

"No fox spirit went after my sons."

"Father," her eldest brother snorted. "You cannot believe he is blessed simply because Master Gao has seen a fox."

Her father straightened to his full height as he took the coarse brush from Zhi Hao's hand. "What I believe is that I must do my duty to the ancestors." So saying, he bent to scrub the stone. But rather than finish the task, he cleaned one small portion. Then he straightened and held the brush out to his first son.

"As must you," he said.

Jian Hong took the tool and did his part, as did her second brother. There was nothing left to scrub then, though her young nephew toddled over and, with his father's help, did his best. With the tomb cleaned, the entire group bowed three times before the women began offering their gifts.

All went in order, save for herself. She watched behind her jade beads as her mother, sisters-in-law, and cousin all presented gifts of food, flowers, and incense. She was saved for last because her offering would be the most auspicious.

While she stood there, her feet aching from the awkward shoes, she was aware of Zhi Hao's gaze on her. Certainly, he kept his head lowered in respect. In this gathering, he was the lowest person, even lower than the retainers, since they were part of the Song household.

But still, she was excruciatingly aware of the way he peered at her at despite his lowered head. Did he look to see if she was in truth a demon? Or was he remembering their nights together? How she had released her chi around his hand, and he, in turn, gave up his own.

Just the memory made her flush with desire. And that was completely inappropriate for the chaste Song daughter who was meant for the emperor. Which meant she had to redouble her efforts to appear demure in every way.

She kept her head down, she performed her kowtows, and she never, ever looked directly at Zhi Hao. She carried her gifts of food to the tomb. She burned the joss sticks and paper. She even recited her best poetry for the ancestors and prayed diligently for success in the Feast of Fertility.

She had just finished her last kowtow when disaster struck.

Chapter Twelve

ZHI HAO COULD not seem to catch the Song daughter's eye. He couldn't see much beneath her curtain of jade beads, and he couldn't tell if she was indeed the woman he'd spent two glorious evenings with. Maybe she was exactly as she appeared: dull, obedient, and chaste to the point of being asexual.

He listened carefully to her recitation of poetry, hoping to recognize her voice, at least. Unfortunately, her voice was demure, but barely audible. Or maybe it was that he didn't hear the commanding tone, or lilting laughter he was used to getting from her that confused him. What he did hear, however, was rustling nearby. Was something moving in the shrubbery? Or was that the wind in the trees?

Then he saw it. A flash of red fur and a thick tail. White teeth and a growl that set his hair on end. Then suddenly, he heard a yelp as a man jumped out from behind a thick group of shrubs.

Zhi Hao reacted before he fully processed what he was seeing. His focus was on the man's sword and the way he seemed to be heading straight for Ling Xin who was still prostrate on the ground in her kowtow.

Whether on purpose or by accident, the man was armed and he could kill. Zhi Hao only had a thick handled broom to use in her defense, but he could wield it effectively. Especially against a man who was looking behind him as if he'd been attacked by a

Mongol hoard.

Zhi Hao used his broom to block the sword. The man hadn't been holding it with much strength. After a few well-placed blows, the man crumpled, his sword clattering to the ground before the earl.

That should have been the end of it. Zhi Hao stood over the man, broom handle at the ready, as the earl bent down to pick up the sword. It was a rusty, chipped thing, and the earl frowned in confusion.

What a bad weapon. A meat cleaver would be better. But before he could say anything, a woman's scream ripped through the air.

It wasn't Ling Xin. She was still straightening from her kowtow. The sound came from the shrubbery all around as a woman burst forth brandishing a kitchen knife. She ran straight for the man on the ground. Others followed, two older boys and several children of various ages.

The retainers handled them easily, knocking them aside with skillful blows. Zhi Hao didn't need to do anything with his broom. It was clear to him that these were no trained fighters. Most likely, these were starving peasants, waiting to steal the food left for the ancestors. The man had burst from his hiding spot because of the red-furred creature who had attacked him, not because he was trying to assassinate the earl.

But what was clear to Zhi Hao was not so obvious to others. And while he waited for the earl to quiet everyone down, he searched the ground for the animal. Could it have been a fox spirit? There weren't that many red-furred creatures alive in the city, and he had seen one three times now in the last week.

But why would a fox spirit attack starving peasants?

Meanwhile, the earl and his sons were quickly containing the so-called attackers. A few of the Song party had screamed during the commotion, but not Ling Xin. She stood quietly nearby, now on her feet and apparently alert.

If nothing else, that confirmed to him that she was indeed the girl he'd met on the wall these last nights. That daring woman would not cry out during an attack. She was more likely to grab a weapon to defend herself.

And indeed, he saw the Song daughter flex her hands as if searching for something to hold, though she quickly stilled the motion beneath her long sleeves.

Meanwhile, the earl was confronting the quivering man at his feet.

"Why do you attack me?" he demanded.

"No, no, honored sir! I meant no harm!" The man had a high voice and obvious sores on his hands and feet. "Please, I was…there was a fox." His voice trailed away already knowing how ridiculous that sounded. But, of course, Zhi Hao had seen it, too.

"You have no reason to be here. This is Song family land. You defile my offering, insult my ancestors—"

"No! No!" the man began, and it was quickly echoed by the others around them.

It didn't matter, though. The earl could not let an insult like this pass without penalty. Zhi Hao could see the regret in the earl's face, but that would not stop him from ordering these poor people killed. To endanger his family during a festival was a serious crime.

And yet Zhi Hao could not let it stand.

"No, no, Earl Song. I'm afraid there has been a misunderstanding. It is completely my fault. These people are part of my family, come to help me clean the tomb. They brought cleaning tools, you see, to help clear away any grime that might remain."

The earl snorted, clearly seeing the lie for what it was. Especially since one of the "cleaning tools" was a notched and rusty sword.

"Your family. This group?" he said.

"Not family by blood, of course. They are part of my…my kindness family."

"Your what?"

"My kindness family. When I arrived in Peking, I grew lost and confused. These people…" Zhi Hao gestured expansively including all eleven of the group. "They helped me find Master Gao's home. And as such—because of their generosity of spirit—they become part of…"

"Of your kindness family?"

"Yes." He tried not to wince, but it was all he could think of in the moment. He knew how ridiculous it sounded, and yet he was already committed.

"I have never heard of such a thing," the earl drawled.

Of course not. Zhi Hao had just made it up. "It is a custom in the south. Begun by the Shaolin monks." Silently, he begged his old teacher's forgiveness. At least, the monk had often taught kindness.

"Is that where you learned to fight? You are a monk?"

"I am nothing so honorable. I was merely a boy among many who was taught by a generous monk."

"Hmmm. He taught you well. You defended me from a sword with nothing but a broom."

It wasn't much of a sword, but Zhi Hao would take it.

"And since you defended my life so ably, I will give you a boon. What is it you want?"

So many things sprang to his tongue. A simple boon would be to discuss the exam that Earl Song had passed so many years ago. Another would be to share an afternoon's tea simply to further the connection for the time after he did pass the exam. He longed instead to ask for his daughter's hand, but that was too far to go. And it would serve no one for him to be so bold.

In the end, he couldn't force himself to select any of those choices. Instead, he looked at the dirty and tear-stained face of the woman who knelt over the man as if her frail body could protect him. He couldn't abandon them to their fate. As far as he could tell, their only crime was being hungry.

"Thank you, Earl Song. You extend me great indulgence. I merely ask that these people be allowed to finish their task here.

While you and your family feast, they will complete the cleaning and defend the tomb from any who would harm it." He looked down at the pair on the ground. "Is that not true?"

"Y-yes, honored sir."

"We will make the stone gleam."

All around them, the eight children and one very old man quickly murmured their agreement.

The earl chuckled, the sound openly mocking. "You claim these people as kin. You, who would serve the emperor, now stoop so low as to claim them?"

Zhi Hao flinched. He knew the trap he was in. No one who hoped to pass the imperial exam could claim any connection with people as wretched as this. Those who served the emperor had to pretend to wealth and status, else they would reflect badly upon the emperor.

But having already defended these people, he could not change his position. They were too wretched, and he knew how perilously close he might be to them one day. If he failed the exam, if he couldn't find students, then he too might be desperately hungry.

Even if it cost him his future, he would not abandon them now.

"They are my kindness family," he repeated. "They are good souls," he said, praying it was true. "It is no crime to be hungry."

"No, it's not," agreed the earl solemnly. "Indeed, some might say it is a mark of honesty." The man shook his head. "Very well. I will allow this kindness kin to defend my ancestors."

Zhi Hao exhaled in relief, but it was a short-lived moment as the earl continued.

"But I will have every one of their names, and each one shall be like a stone around your neck. If they perform their duties poorly, then it shall be you who bears the punishment."

Oh hell. What sort of people he had just tied himself to? Then the earl waved his hand to the whole party.

"Let us leave Ko Zhi Hao to the gathering of names. We shall return home to feast."

Everyone turned, readying themselves to go, but the earl wasn't finished. As his family trailed out of the shrine area, he paused long enough to look back on the wretched group left behind.

"Ko Zhi Hao?"

"Yes, honored earl?"

"See that they dispose of the food properly. I cannot have animals coming to eat it. It would defile my ancestral shrine."

"Of course," he said bowing deeply. "The food will be managed, and the stones kept polished." He would have to return here tonight to make sure of it.

"Good. And once you have written down all their names, bring it to me at my house. Master Gao and I will assess your calligraphy during the feast."

Zhi Hao's head shot up. Had he just been invited to dine with the earl? He couldn't read the truth of it off the earl's face. But beside him, he heard Ling Xin gasp. He wondered if her sound was from shock or surprise, then he saw the slight hop to her step as she filed out of the area with her family.

He still wasn't absolutely sure that she was the woman from his nighttime play, but either way, he could now further his relationship with her family. Perhaps there would be a way, somehow, to keep her away from the Festival of Fertility. If she could wait a year, he would be in a position to offer for her hand.

But first, he had to get the true names of the wretches who now outnumbered him. He hoped they understood what he'd just done for them. Otherwise, he was equally likely to be stripped and beaten for the clothes on his back.

CHAPTER THIRTEEN

L ING XIN QUIVERED in excitement. She and her mother stood behind the women's screen, listening to the men's conversation. It had been the usual fare before Zhi Hao showed up. Talk of medicine from her brothers, complaints about the eunuchs from her father, and the rising price of everything. Behind Ling Xin, her sisters-in-law spoke of their children, their servants, and the rising price of everything.

Ling Xin barely listened, speaking only when absolutely necessary. Her attention was split between her sisters-in-law and what was happening through the screen among the men. Then Zhi Hao entered, and she abandoned all pretense of caring what the women were doing.

She watched as Zhi Hao entered, bowed, then handed her father a scroll, presumably of the names of the people left to defend the Song family tomb. To her delight, her father then offered him a seat at the table.

That was quite a coup. Normally a simple student would not be allowed at a family feast. Ling Xin was very excited to see him sit down, except when all her male relatives began grilling him, as if they were the judges in the imperial exam.

Fortunately, Zhi Hao was able to answer all their questions. And that made her giddy with excitement. Her father had accepted him! That gave her hope for something she should not be thinking. She was meant for the emperor. All her thoughts should be on him.

Nevertheless, a question danced at the back of her mind, pushing forward whenever she heard the deep rumble of Zhi Hao's voice.

What would it be like to marry him?

She had seen what he did at the tomb. She had been encumbered by the damn shoes and half-blinded by the jade beads, but she'd seen it nonetheless. When the peasant had burst out of the shrubbery, Zhi Hao had stepped directly between her and the attacker.

It was only fortune that it appeared he defended her father, but she knew the truth. Every movement he made put him between her and the peasants. He had been protecting her, and she was flushed with heat at that knowledge.

Even her own brothers had never stood in her defense. They'd teased her as brothers do, and she'd given back as best she could. They had a good relationship, but they had never risked themselves to protect her from an attacker before.

Only Zhi Hao had done that. And now he was turning the tables on her father. He was asking questions she barely understood. Things about how the government was run, how an official could best work inside the structure. Details that only one who worked closely with the emperor would know.

And she could tell that her father was impressed.

But then her father had enough of being questioned. He clapped his hands and called for more wine even as he turned to Zhi Hao.

"Are you engaged, Ko Zhi Hao? Is there a bride already selected for you?"

"No, Earl Song. All is dependent upon my passing the exam. And once I have my appointment—"

"You could be sent to the farthest corners of China, you know. If you do only fair on the exam. Enough to pass, but not enough to impress."

Zhi Hao bowed. "I will be honored to—"

"Yes, yes, of course." Her father's eyes glittered from the wine. "But if you did exceptionally well, if you had a man who might ask for you, then you might stay in Peking. Especially if you impress a man who appreciates loyalty and has much to teach an earnest young man."

Obviously, that meant her father. She knew that her father was desperate for a protégé, and that his greatest disappointment was that her two brothers had not passed the exam. Could he be thinking of Zhi Hao? If yes, then everything might work out well! Everything—

"I have a niece visiting. She has a voice like an angel, and she has been trained since her youngest days in how to support an important man. I will call for her. You must hear her sing."

Ling Xin jolted, at once seeing her father's thoughts. He meant to match Zhi Hao with Li Fei! Well, of course he did. Ling Xin was meant for the emperor.

Beside her, Li Fei gasped, her hand going to her throat. Mama also gasped and quickly turned to squeeze her niece's fingers.

"He is a handsome boy and very intelligent," Mama said to Li Fei. "He will make you an excellent husband."

Li Fei nodded, her eyes going to Zhi Hao even as her hands began fluttering. "But what should I sing?"

No, no, no! Panic clutched at Ling Xin's heart. He couldn't fall in love with Li Fei! It would be too cruel. And yet what could she do to stop it? Nothing. Especially since she had no wish to thwart Li Fei's chances.

"Sing the Fan Dance song," she abruptly said.

"What? But then who will dance?"

"I will." She grasped Li Fei's hands and said as much of the truth as she could. "You sing it so beautifully, but sometimes you get nervous." In truth, Li Fei's stage fright had been a problem a decade ago. She hadn't had a problem in years, but uncertainty ran deep and her next words proved it.

"I can do it, but I would prefer to have someone with me,"

she confessed.

"Of course, you can do it," Ling Xin reassured her cousin. "But this way I will be there to take some of the attention. If you mess up, you can blame it on me. Say I missed the steps, and you tried to cover."

Li Fei nodded. "I always do better when I sing for a dancer. I can look at them and match the song to their movements."

"I know. That is why I suggested it," she lied.

"But what about your foot? You said you hurt it."

"My foot is fine." For the most part. "And I could use the practice in front of people, just like you." She squeezed her cousin's hands. "Please, please let me dance."

"Yes, of course!" Li Fei said. "It will help me more than you, but uncle has to agree."

Her mother huffed out a breath, then eyed them both. "You leave that up to me. I shall arrange it. Now quick!" She waved her hands at them. "Get dressed for a performance!"

They rushed off to get their costumes. This was not the first time they had performed together. It was customary for an official to entertain minor dignitaries with music. It was her father's good financial sense that made her and Li Fei his entertainment. They were cheaper than professionals and almost as good.

It didn't take long to get ready. They had already dressed and set their hair for the Chingming festival. All it took was a change in wardrobe complete with the large fans Ling Xin would use during her dance.

Still, they barely made it in time. Indeed, she could already see that her father was flushed from wine and impatience. But he grinned when they entered the room, and soon the wife of Ling Xin's eldest brother was playing the opening notes on the zither.

Ling Xin danced as if she were performing for the emperor himself. She twirled, she stepped, and she used her fans to great effect. She tried not to dance specifically for Zhi Hao. She was not supposed to show preference, but every step, every turn had her gaze searching his face.

He looked pleased, she thought, but it was a polite expression, one perfect while sitting in the house of an earl. It was not the kind of look she was used to receiving from him. In fact, several times she caught him looking at Le Fei rather than herself, and the pique she felt at that almost made her misstep.

When the performance was done, everyone applauded. She looked to Zhi Hao, but his gaze was on Li Fei, his expression almost one of awe. And one glance at her father showed that he was well pleased.

Then the earl grinned at her. "The emperor will adore you," her father said fondly. "Now go rest, my beautiful daughter. Let Li Fei entertain our guests tonight."

And so she was dismissed. There was nothing she could do about it. She slunk back into her room, nearly threw her costume into the trash out of pique, but then settled down. She knew why this was happening. Her father was tasked with matching her cousin with a husband. Who better than a promising student who had already worked extra hard to please him? Father had found a protégé and a good husband for Li Fei all in one stroke.

She should be pleased, but she felt sick at the idea of Zhi Hao doing with Li Fei all the things they had done. She scrubbed the cosmetics off her face with a ferocity that nearly drew blood.

He could not have Li Fei! And she was a shrew to think such a thing. Because if she were destined for the Forbidden City, why would she stop her cousin from catching a good man? An excellent man who defended women and saved peasants.

But now what was she to do? She could still hear Li Fei singing. Indeed, their applause when she finished carried through the whole house. And that made Ling Xin seek her bed.

The men would be drinking late into the night. She would not meet Zhi Hao tonight, even if he banged on her door and begged. So she curled into her pillow and cried.

CHAPTER FOURTEEN

Z HI HAO DID not see Ling Xin that night, not that he expected to. He had seen that as much as she tried to hide it, she had been dancing just for him. That knowledge had him pulsing with desire.

And it told him that she was no fox spirit. She could not hide her passionate nature or her impudent smile as she danced. Not when she flashed him a coy glance or turned to look straight at him.

She was flesh and blood, and she had danced for him. He, who had little claim to title except as the son of the lowest red bannerman. He, who had nothing to recommend him—no wealth, no status, and no job—except for the possibility that he might pass the imperial exam.

Bright, daring, sensual Song Ling Xin had danced just for him, and everyone had seen it.

That, of course, was the problem. Her father had noticed and had dismissed her immediately after the dance. No doubt she would get forcefully reminded that she was meant for the emperor.

Meanwhile, he was given to consider Li Fei. And if he accepted the woman—after passing the exam—then the earl would sponsor him for a profitable position managing China's finances. He had said that exactly and repeatedly.

That was no small offer. Indeed, it was everything he'd ever wanted, wrapped up in a neat Li Fei bow.

He should want it. It was his entire future exactly how he envisioned it. What was one woman compared to all that? Ling Xin was destined for the Forbidden City and there was nothing either of them could do about it.

He would do well to forget her and focus on her cousin. After passing the imperial exam, of course.

Except that night, he dreamed of Ling Xin. And the night after that, he was waiting for her, already in the treetop bower. If she didn't come, then he would know she had accepted the situation. She knew as well as he did what her father had offered him. She knew that he should take it with both hands.

She knew it. And yet, that night, he saw her creep out to the wall and climb up, just as she had done almost every night.

"You are going to marry Li Fei," she said as she settled on the wall facing him. Her words were equal parts accusation and logic. She knew what was best for him, but she didn't like it.

He didn't either.

"You don't deny it?" she challenged.

"Do you deny that you will enter the Feast of Fertility in three weeks' time? That you will attempt to become the next empress?"

She shook her head, and he could see the shimmer of tears in her eyes. "I am not the empress yet."

"And I have not passed the imperial exam yet."

She nodded, and they both fell silent. In the end, she sighed.

"Li Fei is kind and loyal." She sighed. "She will make you an excellent wife."

He didn't mention that what he wanted in a wife was a sense of daring. It excited him, and not just physically. Most girls were trained to be porcelain dolls, and he found them extraordinarily boring.

Instead, he patted her hand. "You are beautiful and smart. You will make an excellent empress."

She smiled then, a little coyly as she looked up at him. "Did you like my dance?"

"It was grace and perfection. I was very impressed."

"So you think it will interest the emperor?"

How he hated his ruler right then.

"Not in the least."

She jolted, clearly shocked. "What? Did I do the steps wrong?"

He gentled his tone. "You know you did not."

"But—"

"Your dance was skillful, graceful, and very proper. I have already told you that proper girls do not interest a man. Not the way you want."

She frowned. "But you liked it, didn't you? You said you were impressed."

He took her hand, gently guiding it with his own. "Ling Xin, I have only to look at you to desire you. The thought of you haunts me so much that I thought you a fox spirit."

"I am not a demon," she said, and thankfully, her voice held humor not annoyance.

"And yet you have bewitched me. We have done nothing improper this night and feel me. My dragon weeps to be inside you."

He set her hand on his organ, and it immediately pulsed into her hand. And true to her daring nature, she did not pull away. Instead, she shaped him with her fingers, toying with his organ through the covering of his pants. And her expression grew wistful as she played.

"If I am selected for the lower harem, I will never bed the emperor. This is as close as I will ever be to a man's dragon."

He winced. "There is always the possibility—"

"No. I have spoken with my father. He came to me this afternoon to discipline me for making eyes at you."

Zhi Hao's body tightened in horror. "Did he hurt you?"

She frowned. "No! He is not a violent man, and he loves me." There was hesitation in her voice.

"What did he tell you?"

"It is what I told him," she said, taking on that empress tone he so adored. "I forced him to tell me everything. I told him that if I am to be locked forever inside the Forbidden City, then I must understand how it functions. I must take any advantage I can, and that starts with understanding what it is like inside."

Smart. But he shuddered to think of what she'd learned. Almost as much as he hated to think of her inside that place.

"What did he tell you?"

"As much as he knows. He admitted, eventually, that the emperor is a man in flesh and blood, subject to the same desires. He says the eunuchs have more control over the harem than he does. And that I must be smart if I want to attract the emperor's attention."

"Did he have any suggestions?"

"No. He will give me a great deal of money to bribe the eunuchs, but beyond that, he cannot help me."

Not surprising.

She sighed. "He still says he has utmost faith in me. He believes I will find a way to catch the emperor's eye. And that I will be empress."

She spoke those words flatly, as if reciting historical facts of no consequence. He ached when he heard it, knowing the cruelty of her position. He could see that she hoped for a different future, but now knew that her father would not budge. She was destined for the Feast of Fertility.

"I am sorry, Ling Xin," he whispered.

"So am I."

They sat in silence for a long moment. He listened to the sounds of the night while he watched her expression shift through anger and frustration to a sad acceptance. In the end, her lips tightened, and she slowly pulled away from him.

"Very well," she said. "I must find a way to catch the emperor's eye. You say my dance will not do it."

"You were very graceful."

"But that is not enough. Teach me, Zhi Hao. Tell me how to

dance in such a way that a man will want to bed me immediately."

He winced. That was no small task. "Are you sure you want
to do this?" he asked. Meaning, he wasn't sure *he* wanted to do
this. It was already taking all his willpower to keep back from her.
How could he teach her a seductive dance without bedding her
then and there?

Damnation, he wanted her!

"I am sure." She lifted her chin in an expression he had come
to know well. It told him that she was determined to walk down
this very scandalous path. And he could not stop her, even if he
wanted to.

"Very well," he finally said. "Master Gao is gone to thank his
own ancestors for last night's benefit. Your father praised him for
his wisdom in bringing me to him."

She nodded. "That was very smart of him." Then she arched
her brows. "But it was your idea, wasn't it?"

He grinned. "Yes. But in any event, his family shrine is a day's
travel from here." He gestured back at his master's house. "It is
empty tonight, except for us."

Then he arched his brows at her, daring her to risk everything
by coming into his home. If they were caught, they could both be
killed. And yet, this night, he could not stop himself from
jumping down into his garden. He held out his arms to catch her.
And then he waited, daring her to commit to this path.

She did. With barely a moment's hesitation, she pulled her
legs over and dropped neatly to the ground. She was strong
enough that she did not need his help, but he caught her
nonetheless, relishing the feel of her body next to his.

She was fit. So many aristocratic women were not. And she
was supple in the way she moved. Dancing must have come
naturally to her for she glided away from him now, making
following her irresistible. If he hadn't felt her body, he would
have thought her a spirit sailing through the air.

But she was real. And now she was headed for his bedroom.

CHAPTER FIFTEEN

Ling Xin was filled with a desperate kind of recklessness. She had no business being in Zhi Hao's bedroom. Indeed, she had no business doing any of the things she was doing, but after this morning's discipline from her father, she was more resolved than ever to complete her training.

Her father had not hurt her. He had restricted her to one bowl of rice until the Feast of Fertility as punishment for being greedy with her eyes. He had seen her looking at Zhi Hao. Fortunately, he thought it was because she had been practicing her feminine wiles on the only available man she had seen in years. He had no idea that she knew Zhi Hao so intimately.

He didn't know that her real punishment was realizing that her future was set. That in a few weeks' time, she would enter the Forbidden City and never leave it again. She would be one of many women among eunuchs. Even if she became empress, she would serve only as bedmate to the emperor and only if she conceived a male child. Every other moment of her life would be restricted, watched, and completely proper.

If she was to ever truly live, ever to enjoy the thrills that Zhi Hao introduced to her, now was the time to do it. She didn't have the privilege of second guessing.

So she jumped down from the stone wall, letting him catch her so that she could feel the hardness of his body against hers, and then she went inside Master Gao's house.

She expected Zhi Hao to take her straight to his bedroom, but he stopped her in the main sitting room. His expression was grim, but one look at his pants told her he was as excited as she was. That was a good thing. So why did he seat himself on a couch and lean back, as if expecting her to entertain him?

"You promised to teach me," she said, her annoyance clear.

"You want to dance in a way that excites the emperor."

"Yes."

He gestured to her. "So dance."

She gaped at him. "There is no music, no costume."

"A courtesan needs none of those things." He grinned. "Hum if you must. And use your hands as if they were fans. I will get the idea."

"But how will I dance differently? You said I bored you before."

His smile turned rueful. "I do not think you will ever bore me, Song Ling Xin." His expression softened. His moods tonight were making her dizzy. "Remember how I made you feel on the wall? Remember how your breasts felt heavy and tight. How your yin cauldron…" He gestured at her belly. "It turned wet and hot."

She nodded, her body reflecting the very words he used.

"Now dance, but with that memory. Accentuate those parts of your body." Then he leaned forward. "Imagine my hands and my dragon in all those places."

"And what will that do?" she asked, not because she thought he would answer but because she needed a moment to think of these things. It was one thing to experience it in the shadows. The way his hands had moved over her breasts and between her thighs. It was quite another thing to dance while thinking of that.

He grinned. "It will make me think of it, too. And if I am thinking it, then I will want to bed you."

She knew he already wanted to bed her, and she wanted it too. But he was teaching her how to seduce the emperor, and so she set her body into the beginning steps of the fan dance.

This was a folk dance, not intended to be erotic. Traditionally, it told stories of heroism. But some fan dances were meant to evoke emotion, and she relied on that now. She began with the movements for happiness and fat contentment, then added the entrance of something frightening. A man who was large and scary.

When she made those movements, she looked straight at Zhi Hao, but instead of suggesting the storyteller was cowering in fear, she changed her expression to one of interest. She thought of how she had spied on Zhi Hao over the stone wall, watching his body in the moonlight and how it made her body swell just to watch.

She didn't know how to show her nipples getting tight or her mouth turning dry, but she used her hands over her breasts, opening and closing them as if they were large fans. She mimicked her heart beating faster as he approached. And she looked right into his eyes as she licked her lips.

It felt crude, but his eyes widened and he shifted in his seat. She couldn't tell if he was pleased or dismayed. She stopped dancing.

"This is awkward," she said. "The dance is supposed to be graceful."

"What would help you?" he asked.

She shook her head. That was the problem. She knew there were ways to entice from across a crowded room, but she didn't know them. She couldn't begin to imagine—

"Let me dance with you," he said. "Let me show you what men like."

She frowned. "Do you know the fan dance?"

"Not in the least," he said with a chuckle. "But I don't need to."

She thought he would stand in front of her, that he would adjust her body the way he wanted her to appear and then step back. That was how all her teachers had instructed her before.

But this was a very different type of instruction.

Instead of standing in front of her, he stepped behind her, fitting his body to hers. He set his arms around her, his hands meeting hers. And he pressed his back tight against her.

So close. So intimate. She felt every part of her liquify at his nearness.

"What are you thinking?" he asked, his words a low murmur against her ear.

"About your exercises. How you fight enemies. How I love to watch you do it."

"Then maybe we should begin with that instead of the fan dance."

"But—"

"Shhh. I will go slow."

It was a strange thing to move her body in concert with another. Not just in concert, but as one being, flowing forward, shifting backwards, turning a slow circle. He was pressed against her back, pushing her into the movements and then supporting her as he pulled her back.

That alone set her feelings soaring. Forward and back, pressing here and cupping there. But when he began to turn her, encircling her and tugging her around, he pulled her off balance, and yet still supported her.

Such strength he had. Such power to move her body as if it were his own.

"Pretend you have fans now," he said against her temple. She felt the movement of his lips against her skin. "I will guide your body. Use your fans to show me where you are aroused."

She jolted in shock. "You want to see… You want to know…'

"Yes and yes." Then he took her hands and pressed them to her breasts. "Here?"

The sensation even of her own hands on her breasts made her body tighten with hunger.

"Tell me, Ling Xin. Where do you feel most alive right now?"

"My nipples," she said. They were tight enough to skate the

edge of pain. And because his hands still pressed hers against her breasts, she moved her fingers in a way that she knew felt so good.

"Yes," he murmured. "You should do that with your fans."

"Open and close them?"

"Yes."

She set her hands to her breasts, opening and closing her fingers as if they were the fans. She felt every shift against her nipples and her body arched without her willing it. But how good it felt to press her bottom against his dragon. She felt it hot and hard just behind her buttocks.

When he pressed back into her, she knew she had done well.

And again, they began to move in that same forward and back motion, pushing and cupping, with the occasional off-balance twist.

"Where do you hunger now?" he asked.

She couldn't voice it aloud, so she arched her back and straightened such that her bottom stroked his dragon. He hissed in reaction, and she felt his hands tremble, but he didn't give way. Instead, he took one of her hands and put it to her lower belly.

"That is where I am aroused," he said. "Show me where you are."

"You know where," she said.

"I do, but this is a dance. You must show me with your hands."

And so she did as he bid, pressing her spread hand lower until she covered her mons.

"Does it throb?" he asked.

Not until he said the word. And so in answer, she opened and closed her hand as if it were a fan.

"This is not a dance," she protested. This was torture with him so close but not touching her the way she wanted.

"What you have done is a dance. Feel how your body moves against me. Remember what is to happen now, so you can imitate it in the future."

She twisted to look up at him while he still pressed into her back. She wanted to ask what he meant, but he did not give her the chance. Before she could do more than turn her head, he slid his hands up her arms and down her front. Within the space of a breath, he took hold of her breasts. His arms surrounded her while he squeezed her nipples hard enough that she gasped.

But, oh how good it felt! That sharp pain made her knees go weak, but she would not leave the circle of his arms. She wanted him around her. She wanted him on her. She wanted—

"Lean forward," he said. "Set your hands on the table."

She had no will to resist. What he was doing was thrilling. She felt so petite in his arms, delicate and feminine against his power. And with her leaning down, her breasts fell into his hands. Such things he did with them. It felt entirely different than it had when she was reclining against him in the tree.

How her body throbbed with each shift of his fingers.

And then she stopped thinking at all as his hands moved from her breasts to her thighs. She wore her usual light nightrobe, the silk flowing about her body. But with her pressed forward, he had room to slide down her back and gather the fabric in his own hands.

"Trust me," he said. "I will not take your virginity."

"I do—" she began, but her words were cut off as he flipped her clothing up over her back. Suddenly she was naked from the waist down.

"You are gorgeous," he said as his hands cupped her bottom. He squeezed the lobes, tightening around them before lifting them up. "I can smell your musk from here," he murmured.

She could smell his. And she could feel his dragon as he rubbed through his pants into the folds of her bottom. She tightened in reaction, pressing backwards, and he groaned in response.

"Yes," he murmured. "Yes, I could give you all my chi right now," he said as he thrust upward. "But not yet. You must share."

She wanted to share everything. Turning slightly, she looked at him from over her shoulder. She knew her expression was coy as she bit her lip and dared him to make her offer her chi. He growled in appreciation.

"You will make me forget to teach."

She shook her head. "I will remind you," she said. "What should I experience now? What must I remember?"

"This," he said. Then he wrapped his arm around her hip and plunged his fingers between her thighs.

She cried out at the invasion even as she spread her legs. He was so hard, so forceful, and she ought to hate it. But she didn't. She wanted his strength inside her. She wanted him to polish her pearl, to thrust his fingers inside her, and to press her down, down, down until she was pinned and he served her from above.

And so that was what they did.

She braced herself, arching her back as his fingers explored her intimate petals. He opened her and thrust inside. His breath was a hot rasp against her back as he plundered inside her. She tried to make sense of what his fingers were doing, but the movement was chaotic, his fingers going everywhere.

She moved her hips, trying to adjust, but he kept her pinned. His weight against her back felt lovely, and the power in his thrust against her bottom let her know that he was as wild as she.

And then he found her pearl. He did no more than push his thumb upward, but she knew what it was now. She ground against him. She felt impaled on his hand with his thumb pushing against her pearl. And she felt him behind her, holding her, surrounding her, and giving her exactly what she wanted.

Up and down, she moved against his hand.

Her back arched. Her pulse beat in her ears.

And then she exploded.

Her body went wild, the waves overwhelming her.

She cried out from ecstasy.

And she rode his hand as long as she could stand it.

Until it was done. Until her body slowed and the waves eased. Until she collapsed forward against the table, and he…

He…

What was he doing?

"There is another way," he whispered against her back. Then he pressed a kiss to her spine, and she felt the fabric of his pants fall away.

"What?" she asked.

"Trust me," he said. "Men like this, too."

Then she felt his dragon at the back of her body. She felt its wet head as it probed her anus.

She had never conceived of such a thing before. Never imagined that…

"You are already so wet," he said, and she felt him take moisture from her pearl and slide it back. Back and…

Inside!

In and out, but not at the entrance that would be checked. Not where her virginity was. But could this be possible? Could this…

He stretched her. He fingered her in the same way he had introduced her to the front entrance. One finger, in and out. Then two. Then more.

Then his dragon.

It was so large.

It would not…

She could not…

She gasped. Her cry filled the room though it was more like a whimper than a scream.

He was inside her. How she had longed for this, but had never imagined it would be like this. Pushing inside, stretching her open. It was uncomfortable, it was hot and hard. And as she adjusted, she began to feel new sensations.

A burn that was sweet.

A pulse that was too much and not enough.

He began to thrust harder now. Not just the tip inside, but more of his dragon. How much more?

He was speaking to her. He was asking how she was feeling,

was this too much, did she want him to stop.

She didn't have words. Only feelings and these were new ones. These were unexpected sensations…desirable sensations.

This was living.

And so she arched her back to accommodate him more. And as he grabbed hold of her hips, she levered up on one elbow.

"Touch yourself, Ling Xin. I cannot reach, but I want to do this together."

Together? Yes.

She knew what he wanted, and she stretched her fingers below. She had done this to herself before. Once he had shown her how, she had experimented on her own. It was never as wonderful as when he stroked her, but it was still good.

And so she explored her own wetness. She found her pearl. And as he began to move inside her, she let his thrusts press her over her pearl.

He was gasping now. His breath stuttering with every thrust.

She was no better. Her whimpers had become cries.

She was so full. So penetrated.

He was so big, and she so alive.

"More," she rasped, barely recognizing her own voice.

"Yes," he echoed.

And then he pounded her.

And she flew.

CHAPTER SIXTEEN

I F LING XIN were a fox spirit taking his yang energy, Zhi Hao decided he would willingly give up all of it. It wasn't merely that her body was made perfectly to attract him. A woman who was both supple and strong had always stirred his desire, but there were many such women in the world.

Ling Xin was more than beautiful. He loved how curious she was, as if she wanted to taste the whole world and she was daring enough to try it. She had not run in fear when the peasants attacked, and once she chose a path, she committed to it. Including the path that had led him to the most explosive release of his life.

And what was she doing right now? She was laying bent over, flat on the table, her breath lengthening into easy rest as she hummed with every exhale. It was a kind of purr that told him she was well content while he pressed tiny kisses to her back.

Then, because he could not prevent it, he slipped out of her. She whimpered slightly at that, but did not move. It was left to him to bring bucket and cloth to clean them both. She allowed his ministrations, smiling as he washed her. And when she was finally set to rights, he was loathe to let her go.

She needed to leave. Every minute that she stayed here with him was a danger to them both. But having experienced her sexual curiosity, he wanted to know more about what else she pursued.

"Does your mother wish you to become empress?" he asked as he guided her to the couch to sit.

She settled easily into the seat, but then obviously relaxed, letting her head fall back and exposing her long, elegant neck. Then she spoke to the ceiling. "When Mama was pregnant with me, she burned many joss sticks praying that I would be a girl. She knew the age of the emperor's son and that a girl would be the right age to vie to become his wife." She smiled. "Of course, they didn't know his father would die young and put him into mourning before his first Feast of Fertility. That gave me extra years to mature, otherwise I would have gone to the Forbidden City very young."

That would be a crime indeed for he never would have met her then. "From your very first breath," he whispered. Such far sighted ambition for her parents, and such a cruel punishment for their daughter.

"Every moment of my life has been aimed for this one goal." She stretched and he watched the glorious shift of her body with growing hunger. "I began to feel suffocated by the time I was six."

"What did you do?" She could not have been climbing walls to entice Master Gao's students when she was that young.

"Lots of things," she answered. "I stole my brothers' books and read them."

"Did you?"

She yawned. "Yes. But only because it was forbidden to me. In truth, they were pretty boring."

"Then what?"

"I explored my father's work, reading scrolls, maps, and accounts." She groaned. "Those account books were the worst."

"So why did you keep studying them?"

"I didn't want to, but my father caught me. He said an empress should have an understanding of all aspects of China. It turns out he knew that I had been reading those forbidden texts all along. Indeed, that was why he had forbidden them."

"But they *are* forbidden to women. Or they are where I grew up."

"They are here, too, but no one cares so long as I don't speak of it." She sighed. "Father said that it would be best that the emperor was surrounded by people who understood the world. That included his wife, even if he never consulted her except to bed her."

He gaped at her. "He said that to you?"

"Many times." She sighed as she shifted on the couch to look at him.

"So what do you know?"

"A little bit of everything. I can run a household, balance the accounts, and manage the servants. I also know a little geography, classic literature, and you have seen me dance."

"You learned all that in secret?"

"In secret?" she laughed. "No! Whenever I was caught in mischief, my father gave me more to study. Mother and her kin taught me the basics of medicine. My father taught me accounts and we often discuss the movement of goods throughout China."

"Commerce," he said softly. "You astound me."

She responded with a quotation, or so it sounded that way given the cadence of her speech, but he didn't understand the words. "What did you say?"

Her eyes widened in surprise. "You don't speak Manchu?"

He shook his head. Though he was a red bannerman by heritage, he'd grown up far from Peking. Few outside of the capitol city spoke the language of the Manchurians, for all that they were the ruling elite. He and most everyone he knew spoke Mandarin. Even Master Gao did not know the Manchu language.

"Ah, well, what I said is, 'If a son is uneducated, the father is to blame.' My father believes that applies to daughters as well. Especially daughters—"

"Who will become the empress," he finished for her.

She nodded, and her expression was sad. Then she frowned. "You should learn the language. Those who take the exam as a translator always get selected. Unless they are very stupid."

He nodded. He already knew that, but he hadn't been able to find—or pay—a tutor. He leaned forward. "Will you teach me?"

She smiled. "I would love to." Then she glanced at the table. "After all, you have already taught me so much."

His body tightened at the memory. "Did I… Are you hurt?"

"Nothing beyond a very pleasant ache," she said, her expression turning lascivious.

"Careful," he warned. "You are not supposed to know about that."

She nodded. "I am very good at hiding what I know. But do you mean that what we did is not in the book?"

He frowned. "What book?"

"Mother said that grandmother was given a book on her wedding day. That I could have it as well—"

"A pillow book."

She looked at him, her expression eager. "Do you know of these books? Do you have one?"

He knew of them. He'd even seen one. But that was not something his tutors thought valuable for him. Besides, boys learned things anyway. He saw the book when one of his friends stole it from his mother's bedroom.

"I don't have one," he said. "I'm sorry."

She sighed. "I fear there is a great deal more to learn. And though I enjoy my education, it will not be enough. I cannot dance for the emperor the way I danced with you."

His heart twisted in his chest at the thought of her dancing for anyone other than himself. But he could not say that. Instead, he leaned forward and gripped her hand.

"Think of what we did when you dance. Let it accentuate your movements. It will be enough."

Her gaze held so many emotions that he could not read them all. Sadness, fear, hope, and much more flitted across her face. "Will it be enough?"

Probably not. But if her father had been planning for her to become empress since before her birth, he would have given many bribes to set her up. Zhi Hao now realized that she might indeed be his next empress.

"I will get you a copy of the book," he promised. He had no idea where or with what coin, but if this was all he could do for her, he would find a way.

"Thank you," she said. "And in return, I shall teach you to speak Manchu. Even if you don't pass the exam this year, you can try again next year as a translator."

He nodded. It was a good plan. But it was also a plan that would take too long. She would be locked in the Forbidden City long before he had the chance to take the exam under a new discipline.

She abruptly leaned forward, the light coming back into her eyes. "Let's begin," she said. Then she began to ask him questions in Manchu.

He fumbled with his answers. He had picked up a little Manchu along the way, so he could answer with his name and his family. But beyond that…

Luckily, she was a patient teacher. And he did his best, even though he was always distracted by the lilt in her voice, the sparkle in her eyes, and the joy in her laughter. How odd that her beauty was lower on the list of things he adored about her. She was beautiful, but now he began to appreciate the whole of her, most especially her mind.

They talked—haltingly—about his family, most especially his uncle who was a eunuch in the Forbidden City. She grilled him about what his uncle did every day and night. Everything she might learn about life in the Forbidden City.

It was her way of trying to learn more about her future. And though he cherished every moment they spent together, this was especially depressing. By the time she yawned for the seventh time, he knew the evening must end.

He switched back to his native Mandarin as he stood up. "I must get up early tomorrow to help Wan Fu."

"Who is that?"

"The man who was startled by a fox at your ancestral tomb."

She straightened, adjusting her hair and her clothing as she moved. Though she had been well covered during his language lesson, she still set everything back in place. "But why do you have to help him?"

"Because he is my family now. I have promised." And because it made him feel good to do something other than hunch over scrolls all day.

"Your kindness family?" There was laughter in her tone. "I thought you made that up."

He shrugged. "I did. But I am still beholden to them."

"But you made it up!"

"And I am happiest when I am doing something good for someone else." Did she not understand? "I'm not taking the imperial exam just to get a good salary. I mean to use my power to help the people Peking has forgotten."

She frowned. "The emperor provides for all."

"Some more than others," he countered. "The viceroys are corrupt. The aid from the emperor does not always reach the people meant to have it."

She nodded, her expression grave. "My father says much the same thing."

"We are alike in that."

"Yes," she said softly. "You are. And now I see that you will pass the exam. I see that you have a determination larger than saving your own family." She took his hand and squeezed it. "You will make a great magistrate or viceroy or whatever appointment you receive."

"I shall be happy to pass the exam first," he said.

And so, walking hand in hand, they moved slowly to the garden wall. She switched them back to Manchu as they moved, speaking in whispers that he could only partially understand.

They hesitated at the wall. He wanted to kiss her. He burned with the need, but he knew if he did, she would end up in his bed.

He would not be able to let her go. And so he helped her stand on the stone he had placed there, then boosted her up.

She scrambled up easily, pausing at the top to look back at him. How she glowed in moonlight. He could readily believe her a spirit. But he knew she was flesh and blood. He had touched her, he had loved her, and now he was seeing her safely home.

"Good night," she said in Manchu. He answered in the same way before he watched her drop down to her garden.

Then he heard her gasp.

Zhi Hao had been about to head to his bed, but he froze at the sound. He was already preparing to leap onto the wall when he heard her speak.

"Baba." *Father.*

Then he heard the slap.

CHAPTER SEVENTEEN

Ling Xin had never known such happiness could exist. Not only from the sexual experiences, but simply being with him. They'd laughed this evening a great deal more than she'd ever done with anyone else.

That was the reason she'd been careless when she'd left him. She hadn't bothered to be quiet. They'd been enjoying each other so much these last few nights, with no one the wiser. Except her father was known to pace at night sometimes. And he sometimes prowled the back garden.

He heard her drop down from the wall. He was barely five feet from where she landed. And then she saw him stare at her, his eyes darting between her and the wall beyond. His conclusion was clear.

She had time to say his name and then he struck—a hard backhand to her face, and her whole body thudded against the wall. Fear coursed through her. But before she could do more than straighten from the wall, she heard another body drop quickly between her and her father.

Zhi Hao. He landed in a fighting crouch on the ground in front of her. But he didn't attack. He slowly stood until he was an effective barrier between her and her father. And then, he bowed respectfully to the man. His words were low, quick, and yet still deferential.

"Do not blame her for my sins. I know you fear the worst, but she is still pure."

"Cur! I trusted you!"

Her father punched Zhi Hao straight in the face. And though she knew Zhi Hao could block it, he did not. He allowed the blow to fall, his head snapping to the side. But when her father meant to follow up the blow, Ling Xin leaped forward. He would beat Zhi Hao to death. She knew the younger man wouldn't raise a hand to defend himself.

"Stop it, Baba!"

She tried to run between the two men, but Zhi Hao caught her and set her aside. It was a quick move and one that her father hadn't expected. He'd been going to grab her as well but caught Zhi Hao instead. And in the pause as they both started to regroup, Ling Xin spoke her piece.

"You want me to be empress, Baba! Then stop this madness!" And when her father raised his fist, she gripped his shirt. "Think!"

It was an aggressive move, one that she'd often seen him do to her brothers. It jerked their heads back and broke their concentration. In this case, she hoped it broke through his rage.

It did not. The man lunged for her, but Zhi Hao was there to protect her. As Baba leaped at her, Zhi Hao twisted him around, quickly pinning the man face down on the ground. Her father roared in protest, but Zhi Hao did not let him up.

"You may beat me all you want, but you may not touch her," he said. And he had to keep repeating it until her father exhausted himself. But in that time, the whole household had roused. Soon they were surrounded by her mother, Li Fei, and several retainers who were quickly shooed back to bed. They didn't leave, though, until Mama crouched down beside her husband.

"You are making this worse," she said. It was her voice that broke through Baba's fury.

The man stilled. A moment later, Zhi Hao stepped back to let her father rise. The man did so with angry, jerking movements. But he didn't attack. Instead, they all glared at one another.

"What is the meaning of this?" her mother asked, her voice low but no less angry.

Ling Xin stepped forward. "Baba thinks something that is not true."

Her father glared at her. "You were over the wall. You were with him!"

"I was teaching him Manchu."

Her father snorted, but Mama looked at Zhi Hao. "Is this true?"

"Yes, ma'am," he answered.

Ling Xin looked to her mother. "I can prove my purity. I can still be empress!" She said the words though inside she tightened with anxiety. She had heard how humiliating the examination could be.

"I will check you myself," her mother snapped. "Why would you go over the wall? You know what could happen!"

She did know. She'd been doing it. "You demand I become empress, but you do not teach me about the things I need to know."

Beside her, she felt Zhi Hao stiffen, but she ignored him. She couldn't look at him when she confessed.

"We have taught you everything!" her father all but roared.

"Not about the Forbidden City," she returned. "You have taught me from the cradle to barter for what I need. I taught him Manchu. He taught me about his uncle who is a eunuch inside the Forbidden City." She threw up her hands as if disgusted, when in truth she was terrified. Her father would be within his rights to kill both her and Zhi Hao.

"And what good—" began her mother, but her father understood.

"What do you know of this eunuch? Will he help you?"

"He is the only contact I have there. And only because I bartered with Zhi Hao for it."

Her father shook his head. "I have given bribes. You had no need—"

"There is need, father," she interrupted. "You know there is."

He was silenced because it was true. Meanwhile, her mother stepped forward to stare hard, not at Zhi Hao, but at Ling Xin.

"You will come with me now," she said, her voice cold. "I will check your honesty."

Ling Xin's face burned at her mother's tone, but she knew it was inevitable. She had transgressed badly, and now she would pay the price. And while she followed her mother into her bedroom, she heard her father give orders to his strongest retainer.

"Take him into my library. If he fights, kill him. I will check his honesty in Master Gao's home."

She shuddered at her father's words, but at least she knew Zhi Hao was safe for the moment. He would not run and if it came to a fight, she had no doubt that he would win. But she could think no more of him as her mother shut the bedroom door and rounded on her.

"Have you lost your mind? You are to become the empress! Why would you risk everything on—"

"How, mother? How am I to become the empress if you do not teach me what I need to know!"

"And what is that?"

Ling Xin swallowed, but she would not be deterred. "Have you found Grandmother's pillow book?"

"How do you know that name?"

She thought the answer was obvious. "I learned it from Ko Zhi Hao."

Her mother's eyes narrowed. "And what else has he taught you?"

So much. "I am still pure."

Mama snorted. "You have never been pure. Always looking where you should not, always questioning things you were not to know."

Ling Xin frowned, wondering at her mother's tone. She sounded like being impure was a good thing. "Mama—"

"Answer me honestly or I swear I will check your body and it will not be pleasant for either of us."

Ling Xin winced, but she knew how to answer. "Yes, Mama."

"What have you done with him?"

"I asked him to tell me how to attract the emperor. Men are not interested in purity."

Her mother crossed her arms and glared.

"I have touched his dragon. He showed me how to caress it."

There was no response, just a narrowing of her mother's eyes.

"And…he showed me how to do the fan dance."

"You already know how."

"Not like he showed me. Not as if I danced for the emperor." Ling Xin's cheeks burned. "I danced as if I wanted to bear his child."

"You do want that."

Ling Xin glared at her mother. Was the woman being purposely obtuse? "Not for political reason," she said. "I danced as if…" She moved to lift her breasts high and swiveled her hips. It was an awkward movement, but her mother's eyes finally widened.

"Oh," she finally said. "He taught you that?"

"He said…" She bit her lip, trying to phrase it politely. "He said that men like breasts. And bottoms. I should emphasize those when I dance."

"I see." Then her mother was quiet for a long time before she arched her brows. "Is that all?"

Ling Xin winced. How much could she say? "He rubbed himself against me, but he did not… We did not…"

"You understand how it is done, yes? I know I taught you that much."

"Yes!" And now she knew a great deal more. "I am still a virgin. I swear it."

Her mother exhaled, her expression pensive. "You did this because I would not give you the pillow book."

She didn't argue. Let her mother believe that was her only motive. "I need to attract the emperor as a man—"

"Hsss! Speak no more of this. Your father will not understand."

Or he would understand. And that was worse.

Her mother continued, her voice tight with frustration. "You walk a fine line, Ling Xin. An empress must be clever, she must be able to deceive, and she must attract her husband as no other. I never wanted you to be empress, but it is the path your father decided on before you were born."

Ling Xin's eyes widened in shock. Her mother had never said this to her before, never suggested that her path was anything but pre-ordained.

"I will tell your father that you are pure. As long as there is hope for you to become empress, he will not kill you." Her mother's eyes were tortured. "I can lose you to the emperor," she said. "But I will not lose you to idiocy. Yours or your father's!"

"Yes, Mama."

Her mother sighed. "You are very lucky that Ko Zhi Hao is honorable. You took a big risk."

She knew. "He is a good man."

"And he is meant for Li Fei."

Those words struck straight into Ling Xin's heart. The pain of it made her gasp, and her mother—no fool—saw the truth.

"Aie-yah, you are smarter than that," her mother moaned. "How much time have you spent with him? You cannot be in love so quickly."

Yes, she could. She was. And now what was she to do?

"Ling Xin! How much time have you spent with him?"

"Enough, Mama," she finally said. "Enough to know he will be a good husband. An honorable husband. A—"

The slap across her face was not as powerful as her father's, but it was hard and it stung. Ling Xin didn't stumble. Her mother didn't have that much force in her. But Ling Xin did cower and as she pressed her hand to her hot cheek, her mother glared down at her.

"You will not speak his name ever again. You will not think of him. And if you do, you will say these words. 'Ko Zhi Hao will marry Li Fei.' Do you understand?"

Of course, she understood. It was the only possible ending to this tale.

"Ling Xin!" her mother snapped.

"Ko Zhi Hao will marry Li Fei." She swallowed. "He will make her an excellent husband."

CHAPTER EIGHTEEN

UNDER ANY OTHER circumstances, Zhi Hao would be intrigued by Earl Song's library. He was fascinated by the maps and tallies everywhere. He had no idea if the earl oversaw all of China's money or just part of it, but the network of information here was stunning. And Zhi Hao wanted to learn everything about it. But not now.

Now, he waited in terror to find out if he or Ling Xin would be killed.

He leaped to his feet when she and her mother walked in. Her face was blanched white, and he flinched to see it. Checking one's virginity had to be a painful and humiliating process, even when done by one's mother. Perhaps even more so then.

He took a step toward her, wanted to say something to ease the pain or even to reassure her. He wouldn't let her father kill her. He wouldn't let any disaster befall her. And privately, he hoped that this ended her chances to become empress. That gave him time and a sliver of a chance to claim her for himself.

But before he could do more than speak her name, her father stomped into the room. He dismissed the retainer with a curt nod, and then he turned to Ling Xin's mother.

"Well?"

"She is pure. She is too smart to be anything else."

Her father grunted, neither acknowledging the truth nor

disagreeing. Then he turned to Zhi Hao. "Your bed is neat. I have not found evidence of your perfidy."

Ling Xin huffed. "Because there is none."

Her father whipped around fast enough that Zhi Hao tensed to save her from a blow. But none fell. Instead, her father bent down until he was nose to nose with his daughter.

"You have been reckless and stupid. You do not deserve to be empress."

"That is not the threat you think it is."

Everyone gaped at Ling Xin. For a woman who had been caught sneaking out, she was remarkably bold. If nothing else, her parents had trained her to be strong, to stand her ground. Indeed, if her color had been pale before, she was now flushed with emotion.

"You dare?" her father rasped.

"Of course I dare," she snapped. "What is an empress but one who dares?"

The words made only partial sense, but her father seemed to understand. But he was not cowed.

"You are nothing without me!" he bellowed.

"And all your plans will come to nothing without me," she countered. Then she lifted her chin, every inch the empress. "Shall we discuss a bargain, then?"

"You go too far," he rasped.

And then Ling Xin did the most extraordinary thing. She looked her father in the eye and nodded. "I do if I am your daughter. But if I am an empress, then I have not gone far enough. Choose, father. What am I?"

Zhi Hao watched with awe as the earl's expression shifted from fury to appreciation. He knew that an empress had to stand tall no matter the provocation, even against her own father. And so his daughter finally earned his respect. But she was still his daughter, and he would demand deference.

"Do not spend coin from an empty purse."

"You have filled my purse, father."

"At least you know who has given it to you."

At that, she bowed, showing that she did indeed know who had trained her to be the magnificent woman she was. Zhi Hao had adored her before. Now he worshiped her. She would make a magnificent empress.

"Very well," her father finally said, grudging respect in his tone. "If I say you are empress, then what should I do with him?"

She turned to him, as did everyone else in the room. Zhi Hao could see the agony in her eyes, need and desire that were quickly suppressed. Did his eyes mirror the same? He certainly felt them.

And when his heart all but broke, she spoke. Two words that shocked him to the core.

"Train him."

"What?" her father exploded.

"Ko Zhi Hao has bargained with me faithfully. He has treated me honorably when…" Her voice faltered a bit. "When he could have taken advantage."

Her father folded his arms and glared at Zhi Hao. "That says he has fear, not honor."

"It was a smart bargain on his part, don't you think?" she continued, dismissing her father's statement with a wave of her hand. "He learned Manchu when he hasn't the money to afford a teacher. And he became friends with the future empress." Her voice didn't waver when she said those words, but her gaze did, flicking to him and then away. "And in return, he told me everything he knew about the Forbidden City. Much more than I had ever heard from you."

There was no accusation in her tone, and yet everyone heard it nonetheless. Her father's eyes flashed hot.

"And for that, I am to train him in the lifeblood of China's commerce?"

"You have two sons in whom you poured your love and training. Neither had the drive to succeed at the imperial exam. Neither could follow your footsteps into the Forbidden City."

"Your brothers have nothing to do with this!"

"My brothers failed you." She pointed to Zhi Hao. "He will not."

"That has yet to be seen."

She arched her brow at him. "I have seen it. I know it. And as an empress, that should be enough."

The words were preposterous, and yet her confidence was so blatant as she spoke that Zhi Hao felt the truth of it. He would pass the imperial exam. He would work diligently for her father. And he would do it because she wanted him to.

Meanwhile, her father rocked back on his heels, his gaze going back and forth between her and Zhi Hao. "What do you feel for this boy?" he finally asked.

She flinched, and he closed his eyes. He did not want to hear what she had to say, either good or bad. Both would break him.

"Answer me!" her father snapped.

She did not. Instead, her mother stepped forward. "It is love. Can you not see it? They think they know what it is."

"Love," he scoffed. "And what do they know of love?"

Her mother rolled her eyes. "What did we know?"

The earl glared at Zhi Hao. "Is this true?"

There was only one answer. He gestured reverently at Ling Xin. "How could I not?"

"Because I say you cannot!"

And now it was Zhi Hao's turn to show his mettle. "Empress or not, I will devote my life to her."

Her father snorted. "Childish nonsense. You are not in love!"

"And yet my vow remains."

The earl paced the confines of the library. He glared at both his daughter and Zhi Hao, grumbling under his breath. He even paused at one point, standing in front of his wife, but the lady said nothing. She merely shrugged. They both knew they could not stop feelings.

In the end, the earl rounded on his daughter. "Here is my bargain with you both." He flicked a dismissive glance at Zhi Hao to focus on Ling Xin. "You will become empress. You will study and practice the virtues."

Ling Xin lifted her chin, her gaze hard. "And in return?"

He grimaced, but he turned to face Zhi Hao. "I will train him. An hour every day, here. If he is capable, then I will accept him as my protégé. Assuming he passes the imperial exam."

Zhi Hao jolted. That was a position that would make his career. It would give him a salary large enough to help his family, to dower his sisters, and to have a wife of his own. Such largess couldn't be ignored. And yet…

His gaze went to Ling Xin's. He would have to give her up.

She returned his look, her expression carefully blanked. She knew—as did he—that so long as she was a virgin, her father would send her to the Feast of Fertility. Short of total disgrace, she could not escape the Forbidden City.

But her father was not done. With a snap of his fingers, he pulled Zhi Hao's attention back. "You will learn Manchu," he commanded. "It is a necessity at court."

Zhi Hao nodded.

"Li Fei will be your instructor."

Zhi Hao winced, but he understood the reason. If he continued be near Ling Xin, he would not be able to resist her.

"And your wife."

His breath choked off. Even knowing it was coming, he could not deny the pain that lanced through him. He looked to Ling Xin, but her gaze was on the floor. But what could they do?

He had to know. He had to know what was the cost of disobedience.

"And if I do not?"

"Then your body will be found in the Yangtze River." The earl said the words with such implacable certainty that Zhi Hao could not doubt it.

Worse, he saw the words hit Ling Xin. She was already shaking her head.

"You cannot kill him. If our love is true, heaven will punish you."

If their love was true? Did she doubt it?

"I will risk it," her father drawled.

The tears in her eyes almost undid him, but Zhi Hao stood still. He would not give in. Not yet. He just needed to think—

"Baba, please," Ling Xin said, her voice filled with pain.

"Are you an empress? Or my child?"

"I am your child," she said, her voice quivering.

"Then you have dishonored me and the family. Do you die with him?"

"You will not kill her," Zhi Hao said. "You are not that cruel a man." It was not his place to say such a thing, but he needed to reassure Ling Xin that her father cared for her.

Unfortunately, he may have misjudged the man because the earl whipped around and grabbed Zhi Hao by the collar. "You know nothing of me!" he spat.

"But I do," his wife said softly. She stepped forward and set a gentle hand on her husband's fist where he gripped Zhi Hao. "Empty threats are beneath you."

"Bah!"

Her father threw Zhi Hao backwards, hard enough for him to land painfully against the desk. Zhi Hao caught himself, but if he had not been a skilled fighter, it would have been very painful.

Meanwhile, the earl turned to his wife and daughter. "Look on my face," he said coldly. "Your brothers have failed me. Since then all my time, my favors, and my bribes have gone to one thing." He pointed at Ling Xin. "For you to become empress. You will not abandon that course. You are my daughter, and as such, you will obey me."

There was no quarter in his voice, no softness in his stance. And then he turned even colder.

"I cannot kill my daughter," he continued. "But I will kill the one who has destroyed you." And with that, he turned to Zhi Hao, murder in his eyes.

So it was to be death then. Zhi Hao tensed to fight. He would not hurt the women. He did not think he could force himself to kill the earl. He would not visit that pain upon Ling Xin. But he could fight fiercely enough that he could escape.

But escape to what? The earl would send soldiers to find him. Even if Zhi Hao could still take the imperial exam, he would never get a good position. Never earn enough to help himself, much less his family.

"Stop!" Ling Xin screamed before the violence began. "Stop!"

Her father straightened, his eyes cold. "Give me your word, daughter. Swear to me upon your family, your honor, and your beating heart that you will do as I say."

She nodded, her face as pale as a shroud. "I will do all I can to become empress," she said, her words ringing hollow. Then her eyes flashed fire. "But you must do all you promised for him. He will be your protégé."

"And he will marry Li Fei."

She straightened, her shoulders looking painfully frail despite her stance. "That is between him and Li Fei."

The earl snorted, as if their wishes made no difference. "We are agreed?"

Ling Xin looked to Zhi Hao and said the words that would seal his future.

"We are agreed."

Pain lanced through him hard enough that it cut off his breath. It was the only choice she could make. The earl was too powerful for either of them to disobey. She had made the bargain she thought would save him.

After all, they'd both known from the beginning that she was headed for the emperor's bed.

And yet...

And yet...

He looked at her and said the words he knew the earl wanted. They sliced his throat even as he spoke them because they were more true than he wanted to believe.

"I wish we had never met," he said. "I wish I had turned you away." He looked to the earl. "I will never risk like that again.

Now that I know the price of failure." Did the man understand what he was saying? Did he know that the pain of giving up Ling Xin would haunt him for the rest of his life?

He couldn't tell, but she seemed to understand. He could see the pain in her eyes as clearly as agony cut through his heart.

He would never risk loving again. Because losing her ended all color in his world.

CHAPTER NINETEEN

LING XIN THOUGHT she knew pain. Training for her dancing had been painful throughout her childhood. The beatings she'd received from her nanny when she'd been willful had been painful. But this pain was of the heart and mind. This pain was of love lost.

I wish we had never met.

He loved her. She'd seen that in his eyes and in his pain.

I wish I had turned you away.

She loved him with a fierceness that burned hotter every day.

I will never risk like that again. Now that I know the price of failure.

There was nothing more to be done. Even if she had a plan, even if she could think of a way out of this agony, he would not do it again. He would not exercise in the garden, even if her father had not set a guard to watch her. He would not find a way to kiss her again, even if he was in their house for more hours now than ever before.

And he would not even look at her though she and her mother were tasked with teaching Manchu to him and Li Fei. That was the most ridiculous thing of all. Le Fei did not speak Manchu, so Ling Xin was forced to be his teacher. She had to see him every day, had to hear his voice. And she had to sit and hear her father's grudging praise when he understood whatever task her father set him.

The days ticked by.

Every one of them, she was forced to see him, hear him, even speak to him in Manchu. All while her heart broke over and over again.

And then it was over. She saw him for the last time, whispered, "I love you," as he left, and then watched the door close behind him. In the morning, she would enter the Forbidden City, never to emerge again.

Misery.

In the darkness of the garden, she turned her back on her packed trunk and began to think desperate, terrible things. Wild schemes, each more fanciful than the last. Crazy wishes that could never come true.

It was late and she was a fool because she was there, hoping to hear the sounds of Zhi Hao's exercise. She wanted, one last time, to hear his breath, to pretend she felt the wind from his blows, and to remember how he'd faced down her father and said that he loved her.

"Do you think me a fool?" Li Fei asked as she sat down beside her cousin.

Ling Xin jolted. "What? No! Of course not."

"Then why do you think I would be content to marry a man who loves someone else?"

Ling Xin looked away, her heart squeezing tight at the thought of Zhi Hao with her cousin. "He is a good man. He will treat you well."

"I do not want 'well.' I want the emperor." Li Fei stretched out her hands. "Everyone thinks that because I am small, I am not fierce. I am, you know. I am strong enough to be empress."

Ling Xin looked at her cousin. "I understand now how you changed. Your lover was killed. Mine is gone from me forever." She looked to the garden wall that separated her from Zhi Hao. "Perhaps I, too, will grow hard."

Li Fei snorted. "I am not hard. I know what I want. Do you?"

"I want him," she said, her voice a bare whisper. "I love him."

Her cousin waved that away with a flick of her fingers. "But do you want to be empress?"

"What?"

"Ugh!" Li Fei groaned as she looked to the sky. "You are too lovesick now to think straight. I, too, spent weeks in grief, but no longer. It is time for you to choose."

This time Ling Xin was the one who scoffed. "Did you not hear? I chose for him to live. I chose for him to thrive with a career and a good wife." Her voice broke on that last word.

"Does your father strike you as a man who can kill?" Li Fei asked. "I grew up in the north. I have seen bandits and know the look of a man who will murder his daughter's true love in the name of ambition."

Ling Xin turned and stared at her cousin. "Your father?"

Li Fei nodded, and her expression was indeed fierce. "*Not* yours. So I ask again, do you want to be empress?"

"No!" The word burst out of her. It had been building for years, but now it crystalized into a statement that would infuriate her entire family if they'd heard. "I do not want to live in the Forbidden City. I do not want to watch for daggers in every shadow. And I certainly don't want to seduce anyone but Zhi Hao!" She dropped her head into her hands and spoke through the tears that flowed so easily these days. "But what can I do? I leave for the Feast of Fertility tomorrow."

"And he leaves for the imperial exam." Li Fei gently pulled on Ling Xin's shoulder until they were once again eye to eye. "Can you not think of a way that all three of us may get what we want? With a little daring, for which you are well known."

She looked at her cousin, confusion and a surging hope at war with each other. None of this made sense. What could her cousin have planned? And yet, seeing Li Fei now, she abruptly realized the woman was much more devious than she'd ever imagined.

"I...I do not know what you are thinking," she finally said. Her mind was filled with longing and had no room for plots. She was lost and filled with the memory of him saying that he wished they had never been together.

And then she heard a raspy bark and jerked around to look for the source. There! On the wall inside the bower where Zhi Hao had first stroked her to ecstasy. There, she saw two black eyes and a hint of red in the shadows.

"A fox," she whispered.

"What? Where?"

But when Ling Xin pointed, the animal had disappeared. And so as her hand slowly lowered, she knew the truth.

"It was the fox spirit. And it was annoyed with me."

Li Fei peered into the darkness, her words coming out with quiet urgency. "What do you think that means?"

Ling Xin knew she was making up what she wanted to believe, and yet the fox *had* been there. And if it was giving her a message, then she would grasp it with both hands. "That Zhi Hao and I were chosen for a reason. The fox has been there every time we…we became close."

"You think it is urging you to boldness?" her cousin pressed.

"I do." She turned to Li Fei. "What is your plan?"

Li Fei's plan was simple, though very difficult to enact. Ling Xin was to leave in the morning in a palanquin. The family had arranged for a great show of dismay with mourners and heralds wailing the family's grief at losing so perfect a daughter.

Once in the palanquin, Ling Xin would switch places with Li Fei. They would change clothing and do Li Fei's make up in the closed litter. Then Ling Xin would slip away in a peasant's garb, pretending to be a child come to see the display.

All she needed to do then was make her way to the inn where Zhi Hao was staying, marry him, and ruin herself, not necessarily in that order.

Li Fei assured her that her father would relent eventually. Ling Xin would have the happy marriage with the man she loved, and Li Fei would capture the emperor's regard and become empress.

The difficulties in executing the plan were myriad. Fortunately, Li Fei had figured out all the details, including how she would use the bribes her father had spent for Ling Xin. They were cousins, after all, and the moment she mentioned the earl as her uncle, the bribes would transfer to her since Ling Xin would not be there.

As for tomorrow morning, when Ling Xin would be leaving for the Forbidden City, Li Fei knew how to fake an illness, ensuring that everyone would leave her alone to rest in the dark. Everyone would think she grieved the loss of her chance, since it was well known that her family had planned for her to compete at the Feast of Fertility.

It sounded complicated, but Li Fei was adamant she could do it. More importantly, she had already gotten the costume for Ling Xin and the direction of the inn where Zhi Hao would be staying before the exam.

All they needed now was the will to try something so daring.

And daring was something Ling Xin had in abundance.

IT DID NOT go off as planned, but it was close.

They were caught by the porters carrying the palanquin. It took nearly all of their money to buy the porters' silence. Worse, the bearers refused to wait outside the Forbidden City with Li Fei because they would not give generosity to loose women. They left Li Fei in the line of contestant palanquins to suffer in the coming heat.

Li Fei swore she didn't mind. And then after a quick hug, she bid Ling Xin away to find her own fortune with the man she loved.

All that was left was to get to the inn where he rested.

On the opposite side of Peking.

CHAPTER TWENTY

Z HI HAO SAT on his narrow bed, his head pounding while his heart felt like a leaden weight inside his chest.

He had tried to forget Ling Xin. That had been especially difficult while spending hours every day inside her house. It had been worse when she had instructed him in Manchu.

And every day, he told himself it would get better. She was destined to be the empress. His future depended on him pleasing Earl Song and accepting Li Fei as his wife.

He did his best not to look at Ling Xin. He would not think of her, he would not want her.

It didn't work.

And so in the last days before he headed to the imperial exam and she to the Feast of Fertility, he racked his brain for a solution. He'd planned all sorts of raids where he grabbed her and ran off to the farthest corners of China. He'd thrown himself before Lady Song and begged for a boon. He'd even burned joss sticks to the fox spirit who haunted him, all to no avail.

He found no solution. Especially since he couldn't seem to get past the fact that she'd chosen to be an empress over being with him. He knew she'd done it to save his life, but still, it hurt.

Yet what man took away a woman's chance to be empress? A woman who had spent her life and likely a great deal of her father's fortune in pursuit of that goal.

Except he knew that was her father's goal. He knew Ling Xin loved him. She'd said as much. And yet what could he do?

Nothing.

Perhaps if he passed the imperial exam, he would eventually have enough gold to buy her out of the harem. Assuming, of course, that she did not make it to empress.

So many questions, so few solutions.

None, to be exact. His only hope was to pass the imperial exam and pray some twist of fortune appeared in the future. Something—anything—that might turn things in their favor.

He was burning his last candle in study when someone knocked on his door. It couldn't be Master Gao. The man was almost as nervous as Zhi Hao and had gone to bed early with a bottle of plum wine.

But when the knock persisted, he grumbled as he hauled open the door. He didn't hide his rancor when he growled, "What?"

The person in front of him recoiled at his sharp tone, taking a step back before exhaling in obvious relief.

"Thank heaven I've found you!"

It took a moment for Zhi Hao to focus. The person in front of him wore coarse clothing and a heavy scarf about her face and shoulders. It was a woman, that much he could tell. And then he saw her eyes.

It couldn't be.

"Ling Xin?" he whispered.

"Let me in!" she said, abruptly shoving him aside to enter his room. Once there, she pulled off her scarf and used it to wipe her face. "You have no idea what I've been through today!" Then she turned to him, her smile radiant. "But it's all over now. I've finally found you." She wrinkled her nose as the singing from the taproom grew louder. "Could you not stay in a less rowdy inn?"

"It is the night before the imperial exam. The masters are celebrating."

"Celebrating what?"

He shrugged. "Getting rid of their students."

She chuckled, dropping down onto his bed with a groan. "My feet ache. I have walked across Peking this day. Twice, I think." She smiled at him. "I got lost twice, but I am finally here." She grinned.

He couldn't believe it. After all of his fruitless wishing and planning and praying, how could she be here?

He dropped down to his knees before her, barely daring to touch her. But when he did, she felt solid beneath his hands. As if she was truly here.

"How?" he whispered.

"Li Fei doesn't want to marry you."

He started, then abruptly laughed. "I don't want to marry her either. Shouldn't you be in the Forbidden City?"

"She took my place. And I am taking hers as your wife." Her eyes flashed a moment of uncertainty. "That is what you want, isn't it?"

"More than anything, but..." His voice trailed away. "You were to be empress!"

She shrugged. "I don't want to be."

"But you swore on your honor, your family's honor. Even your beating heart!"

Her expression darkened. "Then I am dishonored. I do not care."

"Ling Xin," he whispered, knowing what her decision had cost her. She might make light of it, but she had thrown everything away in coming to him now. "Why have you done this?"

"My father had plans for my brothers—he set out their course from their earliest moments. But they chose a different path. Am I not allowed to do the same?"

"They failed the imperial exam."

"So, give me the exam. I will fail it, too."

"Ling Xin," he said, straightening until he faced her on the bed. "Can this truly be what you want?" Could *he* be what she really wanted?

She touched his face, stroking the hard cut of his jaw. "I am here, aren't I? I have chosen you." She pressed a tender kiss to his lips, then drew back. "What do you choose?"

Her. A thousand times, her. "I fear you will regret this. I fear you will regret *me*," he said, his gaze landing on his neat pile of inkstone and brush to take with him in the morning. "What if I do not pass the exam?"

"What if my father turns into a monster, finds me at this inn, and drowns me in the Yangtze river?"

He gasped, leaping to his feet as if her father were at the inn's door. "Is that possible?"

She shook her head, but her words weren't as reassuring. "I don't know. You had best ruin me completely before he arrives."

He gaped at her. She didn't mean…

She sighed as she got up to stand directly before him. "Take my virginity, Zhi Hao. We can marry in the morning."

"I must take the exam in the morning."

"After the exam, then."

"I am to report to your father the very next morning." He rubbed a hand over his face. "He will kill me for this."

"Well, we'll say our vows between the exam and the killing." She grinned. "I do not know what is to come, but I have not risked everything, tromped across Peking, and shown up at your door looking like this, just to have you not finish the job."

He shook his head, completely amazed by her. "Finish the job," he echoed.

"Take my—"

"Yes, I know what you meant." He ran his knuckles down her cheek. "I am nothing compared to you," he said. "But in this and for the rest of my life, I shall do my very best for you."

Her eyes widened, and he caught the shimmer of tears in them. "Is that a vow?" she asked.

"It is."

Then he kissed her. And she opened herself to everything. Not just to what he did, but to his heart until it seemed hers beat in the same rhythm, the same breath, the same place as his own.

At that moment, all his worries and fears—and there were many—faded away.

CHAPTER TWENTY-ONE

AT LAST, LING Xin could do everything she wanted with Zhi Hao. There was no turning back, and she gloried in the fact that finally, amazingly, she had taken her life and her lover in hand.

Quite literally.

While he devoted himself to kissing her, to thrusting into her mouth, dueling with her tongue and even teasing the roof of her mouth, she shed her top. It was a relief to get the coarse material off anyway. And when his hands trailed lower along her neck and sides, he abruptly froze.

"You bound your breasts? Why?"

"Li Fei thought it would be safer."

He nodded, though his expression was troubled. "You took a huge risk," he murmured. He hooked a finger underneath the tie and quickly unknotted it. Then he held the silken end of the wrap that bound her and shook his head. "I cannot think you are real. Perhaps you are truly the fox spirit come to tempt me away."

She lifted her hands as if to surrender. "You are worth it, Zhi Hao. As am I."

His eyes widened, and his breath seemed to stop.

She smiled. Had no one ever told him how special he was? She was glad she was the one who had seen his worth.

"But I haven't passed—" he began.

"Enough doubt. Tonight, we celebrate us." So saying, she lifted her arms and allowed him to unwind the binding.

She thought he would go quickly. Indeed, his hands were shaking with urgency. But he still pulled the fabric away in slow circles around her. He didn't move except his hands, and she could do nothing but stand in the circle of his arms and let the fabric fall away.

By inches, it seemed, her breasts were released. And when she could take a deep breath again, his gaze slid to her chest before he reverently began to stroke her flesh.

"So beautiful," he murmured as he tossed aside the silk so he could cup her with both hands.

She closed her eyes, feeling the size and the heat of his hands. "So good," she murmured as she arched into his hold.

His hands began to shape her, and then he moved his thumbs across her nipples. His hold wasn't tight. Indeed, she wanted more of him, more strength, but this gentle rub was maddeningly erotic. As if he touched the most fragile of things.

On it went while she tingled from his touch until finally, she could not stand it anymore. She gripped his face and kissed him hard, this time plunging her tongue into his mouth, demanding more from him.

Breaking from the kiss, he bent down and scooped her up. She thrilled as his muscles rippled against her body, but he was still wearing a shirt, and she wanted to feel his skin.

He carried her quickly to his bed. It wasn't more than two steps, then he set her gently down. She was pulling at his shirt, barely restraining herself from ripping it off him. He chuckled as he straightened, stripping it off with swift movements.

Heaven, she loved looking at his body. In the flickering candlelight, he appeared more spirit than man. But then he stripped out of his pants, and she knew he was flesh.

His dragon sprung up thick and hard, and this time she wasn't shy about touching it. He hissed as she wrapped her fingers around it, but his face showed bliss. Then she began to stroke it, slow even pulls while she watched his face.

Then she had an idea.

"My mother gave me the pillow book."

He jolted. "What?"

"This morning before I left." She grinned. "I had a little time to study it before we made it to the Forbidden City."

She was still stroking him, and he clearly was having trouble focusing. "What?"

"There is a picture in it," she said. "I want to try it."

And so saying, she set her mouth to his dragon. This wasn't the position in the book, but it was the beginning of it. And from his reaction, this was good enough.

She felt his buttocks flex as he began to push into her mouth. His breath was ragged, and his hands trembled along her back. Then abruptly, he pulled back.

"No," he rasped.

She looked up, confused. "But—"

"You first, my love. You first."

She flushed, feeling the heat of his words filling her whole body. He'd called her his love. And while she gloried at that, he gently stripped her of the rest of her clothing.

She was naked now as she'd never been before in front of him. She might have felt self-conscious, but he didn't give her time for doubt. His eyes raked her body, and then his hands followed wherever his gaze roamed.

Her breasts. Her waist. And then her thighs as he pulled her knees open.

Was it time now? Would he enter her and take her virginity?

She felt her belly tighten in anxiety. She trusted him completely, but the taking of her virginity would be new. She'd been told it always hurt.

And while she was fighting her nerves, he slid his hands up her thighs and pressed his thumbs between her folds.

"So wet," he whispered.

She didn't answer. She couldn't as her back arched and her

legs widened until she was completely open to him.

She heard him inhale deeply, his eyes glittering as he said, "I love your scent." Then he maneuvered onto the cot, much too low to use his dragon.

She frowned as she pushed up on her elbows. "Wha—"

Her word was cut off as he set his mouth between her thighs. The things he had done in her mouth, he now did between her thighs. He swirled his tongue against her pearl, he thrust it deep inside her, and he stroked and teased and explored as if she were the most delicious treat he'd ever tasted.

And she flew.

Every stroke, every press, every thrust ratcheted her higher. She went wild beneath his tongue, but he held her down with his hands. Her belly quivered, her breath hitched, and then…

He sucked on her pearl.

She exploded.

And soared.

And while she was still bucking with every wave, he quickly climbed onto the cot. He kept her legs spread with his knees as he lowered himself on top of her.

The waves were barely eased. She was still soaring with the contractions. But she had enough breath to look at him and whisper his word back to her.

"Love."

"Love," he returned.

And then he thrust.

There was the pain of penetration. A sharp bite of stretch. Wet as she was, he was still big. But that sensation only threw her higher in delight.

She lifted her knees, gripping him as he held still, his eyes dark and troubled.

"Ling Xin?" he whispered.

She smiled at the nervous note in his voice. Did he worry for her? He shouldn't.

"More," she whispered.

As his expression lightened, his body began to move. In and out. He thrust and withdrew with every breath.

Oh how she loved this. She wanted him working inside her. She wanted to be split open.

He moved faster then. Harder against her.

She arched to take every impact.

She wanted…

Faster…

Yes!

A last hard thrust, and she felt him erupt.

And once more, she flew.

CHAPTER TWENTY-TWO

Z HI HAO'S MIND came back to him slowly. His body was sated, but the scent and feel of Ling Xin beside him roused him better than strong tea. He had rolled off her and gathered her against him, but already her heat was making his dragon swell.

So sweet.

And she was his.

"I cannot believe you are here," he whispered.

"I cannot believe people don't do that every second of every day."

He grinned, his pride swelling along with his dragon. "I shall try to keep you satisfied."

"And I shall serve you and your children forever."

He smiled. Were those their wedding vows? It felt like it. But there were details to figure out before they could have the ceremony for real. And an exam to pass as well.

"First, tell me how do you feel? That was your first time. Are you hurt?"

She blinked as she adjusted to face him directly. "I feel wonderful." Then she began to move against him, pulsing with her hips while his dragon roared in his mind.

"Wait!" he gasped. "We must talk. Why did you decide to give up your chance at being empress for me?"

"There was no assurance that I would be selected," she said as she propped herself up on one elbow. "But even if I was, that is not the life I want."

He couldn't believe it.

"Still, it is a lot to give up," he said.

She idly traced his chest, teasing his body until his dragon was bobbing with desire.

"I have heard my father speak of the emperor many times. He says that the man is a spoiled child who hasn't learned how to rule effectively. Worse, he has never been taught to listen."

Ling Xin pressed a finger to her lips, warning him not to repeat her words.

"He would not have said that out loud."

"He did. But only at home, and only when he was livid after some decision that made everyone's life difficult." She shrugged, causing her breasts to bob and his gaze to shift. "But the bigger problem, according to my father, is the emperor's lack of decisiveness. The bureaucracy at court is stifling."

Zhi Hao leaned forward to press kisses to her forehead. "I have heard that is true," he said against her skin.

"So why would I want to live in that place? Why would I want to marry a foolish boy who never listens?"

"But that is the court side of the Forbidden City. The private side will be—"

"Different?" She scoffed. "It will be worse."

He couldn't deny it. So many women fighting over one man could get ugly. He dropped his forehead to hers. "But what am I compared to the emperor?"

"You are smart, you know how to listen, and…" She reached down to stroke his dragon. "You love me."

He did. And because he loved her, because he could not get enough of her, he gently urged her up onto her knees. And from there, he guided her to straddle him.

She slid down onto him, her sigh of delight flowing from her into him.

"I like this," she said, as he began to thrust gently upward. "I think it is in the Pillow Book, too."

It probably was.

"There are other things in the book," she murmured as she began to ride him. "Things Li Fei didn't believe would be pleasurable."

He arched his brows.

She grinned down at him. "I think she's wrong."

Then she leaned forward, and he couldn't stop himself. Without willing it, his hands went to her breasts. He grinned, thinking of all the different positions they would explore.

"I want to try them all," she said. "Every page."

His tempo was speeding up. She was keeping his movements shallow, though she began to squeeze him every time he tweaked her nipples. And her skin was flushed rose gold in the candlelight.

"I must honor your father's wishes," he said, wishing he didn't need to say these words. "I must honor your wishes," he continued as his thrust grew stronger. "And I want to honor my own."

She grinned. "So much honor. What will you do?"

He didn't know. And he was fast losing interest in the question.

She was moving more on top of him. Her breasts gave him such delight, but his hands moved between her thighs to where they joined, he inside her.

He adjusted his hand, letting his thumb settle at the base of his dragon. He let her set the tempo. He let her bear down or not. And he enjoyed every second.

She understood her body better now. She knew the feelings of ecstasy and knew the way to reach it. Still, it delighted him to see her movements slow. She ground down on him to please herself. And then she decided when to go faster while his eyes rolled back in his head. Such pleasure from one woman!

She alternated, slow and fast, grinding and pistoning, until he was as frenzied as she was. When he could stand it no more, he flexed his thumb against her pearl.

She cried out in shock, and he thrust hard.

Heaven!

HE LEFT HER before dawn. His body ached, but his mind was clear. He would pass this exam if his life depended upon it. Because it did.

He could not take care of her if he didn't pass. He could not face her father if he did not pass. He could not face her every day knowing he had ruined her if he did not pass.

And so he sat for his exam—three days and two nights in an empty cell—and he prayed she would be waiting for him when he was done. He'd given all that was left of his money to the innkeeper to pay for her room. And he'd given her all his food— meant to sustain him during the exam—so that she need not leave.

He didn't want to think about the dangers she would face, a sheltered girl in Peking alone for three days. He left her a note, begging her to stay in the room. And then he could think of her no more.

All his mind, body, and soul set itself to the task of passing the imperial exam.

CHAPTER TWENTY-THREE

Z HI HAO EMERGED from his exam cell exhausted, hungry, and thinking only of finding Ling Xin. He was unsteady on his feet and had no money to hire a rickshaw to take him to the inn. Master Gao had returned to his home, unwilling to wait three days for the exam to end.

And so Zhi Hao stumbled forward, pushing himself to run despite his exhaustion. He had to know if she was safe. If she was still there. If all of it had been real or a fever dream the night before an exam.

He made it to the inn, ignoring all the well-wishers gathered to greet the students. He rushed up to his room and…

She was there.

She sat at the desk, reading one of his study scrolls. And when she looked up at him, her face lit up with joy. He fell forward at her feet. Dropping his face into her lap, he breathed her in, and he thanked heaven for her. Nothing more. Just her.

"How did it go?"

He shook his head. He didn't know. He couldn't think. All he could do was hold her legs and rest in her lap.

"You must be tired."

He shook his head.

"Hungry?"

Well, yes, he was that.

She lifted his face up to hers. "I have found a way for us to marry. I have everything ready. If you feel up to it, we can get some food on the way."

He blinked up at her. "You don't want to wait? Until we find out—"

"Today, Zhi Hao. I will wait no longer to be your wife."

And so it was done.

He followed her without question. Later, he would ask for details on how she had arranged it. Had she hoarded all his coins? Had she eaten nothing? Where had she found the most delicious bao in China?

Eventually, she explained that she'd met the innkeeper's wife when the lady came to clean the room. Together, the two women had planned it out, and Ling Xin's jade comb paid for everything.

For now, he cared only that the magistrate was kindly, and their vows were traditional. By the time the sun set, they were wed.

That night—back in the same inn—they looked together at the Pillow Book and chose their night activity. Then in the morning, they rose, bathed, and headed out together to face her father.

CHAPTER TWENTY-FOUR

LING XIN WAS smiling when they arrived at the gates of the Song household. She was flush from the success of her plans and the joy of being wed to a man she loved. When the cry went up as they entered, she was thrilled to see her mother run down the walk toward her.

Her mother never ran, but she did now, rushing forward to embrace Ling Xin as if she had thought her dead. And apparently, they had.

"Thanks, she lives. Thanks, she lives. Thanks, she lives."

"Mama, I am fine. Better than fine. I am happier than I have ever been before."

Her mother pulled back, searching her face and then staring hard at Zhi Hao. Contrary to Ling Xin's mood, Zhi Hao's expression had become darker with every step toward her home. He was grim now as he bowed to her mother, and his body was so rigid, Ling Xin feared he would break with the movement.

She had been looking at her husband, so she hadn't seen the blow coming. An open-palmed slap from her mother, not to Zhi Hao who would usually get the stinging reproach, but to herself, with enough force that she stumbled.

Zhi Hao caught her and quickly placed himself between her and her mother.

"Blame me, Lady Song. I am—"

"Not to blame," Ling Xin interrupted. "I did this. He knew nothing of it until I arrived at his door."

"How could you be so cruel!" her mother snapped. "We did not know what had happened to you. We thought you dead by your cousin's hand!"

Ling Xin reared back. "You thought Li Fei had killed me?"

"She took your place. Father discovered it the moment he went to work, but he could not ask. If we were wrong, she would be killed. And yet, he still considered it."

"Li Fei could not kill anyone!" Ling Xin said firmly. At least, she didn't think so. What exactly did she know of her surprisingly devious cousin.

"Then what were we to think? With no word from you and no one knowing what had happened." She gripped her daughter tight. "Why didn't you leave a note, you foolish, idiot child?"

Because a note would have been found too quickly, and there was no one here she could have trusted to delay delivery. But she couldn't say that, so she bowed her head and begged forgiveness.

"I was thoughtless, Mama. Pray forgive me."

Her mother sputtered in her fury, but Ling Xin knew the woman well. She would forgive her child eventually. If not in a few days, then when the grandchildren came.

That settled things with her mother, but her other parent was the one who mattered most, especially to Zhi Hao. Earl Song held Zhi Hao's future in his hands. Even if Zhi Hao passed the exam, the earl could banish him to the farthest corner of China. And he could send Zhi Hao away without his wife.

So when they saw the earl coming into the front courtyard, both Ling Xin and Zhi Hao dropped to their knees in a kowtow. Three times they bowed. Three times, Ling Xin prayed for her father's forgiveness. She remembered now how devastated he was each time her brothers failed the imperial exam. She knew he wondered if they had failed it on purpose.

And now she had done the same, throwing away her chance to become empress because of love.

Did he know how sorry she was to disappoint him? Did he know how happy she was to be with Zhi Hao?

She raised her head. Her father said nothing.

Zhi Hao did the same. Her father said nothing.

And then together, they found their feet. It was a breach of protocol. Tradition said they should stay prostrate until the earl told them to rise. Worse, tradition said she wait for him to speak, but she could not.

He was the man who had bounced her on his knee. He was the one who had praised her mind, and taught her to stand tall. And he was the one who'd once said he loved her.

"Father. Baba. You are a great man with a brilliant mind and a far-seeing gaze. And though I be a woman, you guided me until I could do the same. I still have much to learn, but in this, I saw further than you." She grabbed Zhi Hao's hand. "I saw that love is greater than any emperor or even a brilliant father. Love is what I chose. And I hope that you love me still."

He didn't answer her. His gaze flicked away from her to stare at Zhi Hao. "You did this, despite everything I offered?"

Zhi Hao dipped his chin. "Women are not like shoes, easy to exchange one for another. You raised the most amazing woman I have ever met. How could I give her up, even for everything you offered?"

Her father grunted. "Pretty words. How will you support her?"

"I hope you will honor me with a position. I would learn from you. But if you do not..." He looked at Ling Xin. "I have sworn to honor her. I will find a way, even if I walk the mud-banks of the Yangtze River."

Her father snorted. "That is a hard life."

"She is worth it."

Her father walked directly up to Zhi Hao and met his eyes. Zhi Hao did not flinch. Then her father turned to her.

"Love, huh?"

"Yes, Baba. Love."

"Then let me hear you say it. Let me hear the words that married you two souls despite the dictates of a father and the temptation of an empire. Let me hear those words so that I may see that you mean it."

Startled by what he said, they both stared at him and then abruptly turned to one another. Never before had Ling Xin heard her father's voice so rough, nor seen his face so rigid with emotion that she could not read him.

But when she looked at Zhi Hao, all of that faded away. She saw only her husband, and he was smiling at her.

"I love you," he said. "I swear my heart and spirit to your benefit and that of your family. Forever."

"I love you," she answered, "I swear my heart and spirit to your benefit and that of your family. Forever."

They were not words of any ceremony she knew, and yet they flowed easily from her lips. And when the words were done, they inched closer to one another. A kiss was the most natural end to such an exchange, but her father prevented it.

He grunted and set a hand to Zhi Hao's chest.

"You think to convince me with pretty words?"

Ling Xin smiled. She heard the change in her father's tone. Like Mama, he would grumble, but they had won.

"He could recite wedding poetry, if you like," she said. "I could as well."

"You have the audacity of an empress, but you are not she."

She knew it. "You gave it to me. I am not one to return a gift from my Baba."

"Ugh," he growled. Then he pointed at her. "You will go to your room and figure out the auspicious days for your wedding."

"But we are already—"

"Tss!" her mother hissed. "You are not wed yet," she stated flatly. By which, she meant that any Song daughter's wedding would be full of pomp and circumstance.

"And you," her father continued as he pointed at Zhi Hao. "If you did not pass the imperial exam, there will be no wedding and no happiness for you."

Zhi Hao bowed to the earl. "I understand."

And so did Ling Xin. She understood that her father loved her and would not harm the man she chose. The man she loved. The man who was right now bowing deeply to her father, but shooting her a surreptitious grin as he stayed prostrate.

EPILOGUE

H E PASSED THE exam.

Indeed, with Baba's sponsorship, Ko Zhi Hao was soon established in the financial section of the government. It was after his first day at work that Baba gave him the highest compliment that she had ever heard him say.

"Your husband understands systems," he said. "Numbers can be taught, but systems are the mark of a gifted student. He has a gift, and I am well pleased."

They were married (again) a week after his exam results arrived. That was a long enough delay that his family had time to travel to Peking to attend. The rituals were observed, the banquet a delight, and finally, Ling Xin and Zhi Hao were wedded and bedded in a proper fashion.

There was no period of isolation for a honeymoon. There was only one night in a private suite before they returned to their place in the Song household. Zhi Hao did not have enough salary yet for an establishment of his own, but it wouldn't take long. He continued to impress her father and advancement was assured as long as he remained loyal to his wife and her family.

"And with such a wife," he whispered to her, "how could I ever imagine doing anything else?"

It was evening on their third night in the Song household. They were walking through the back garden, meandering openly here for the first time.

"Will you exercise again for me?" she asked as they neared the place where she had first climbed the wall. "I want to spy on you again."

He shook his head. "Your father has me working so hard, I haven't the strength." He pulled her in tight for a kiss. "Though you are the one making me so exhausted every night."

"You are the one who promised we could explore a new page every night."

"I suppose I am," he said as he trailed his hands down her back.

She shivered with delight, as she always did when he got that look in his eye. And then she rubbed herself against him in the way that made him shiver in turn.

"I cannot believe this is my life now," he murmured against her temple. "How did I get so lucky?"

"I wish there was a way to thank Li Fei," she said.

"There is no way to get a message inside the Forbidden City. Not now."

She knew it was true, but she ached for it anyway. "I wish we knew what happened."

"We do know," Zhi Hao said. "She got her wish."

It was true, in part. The Feast of Fertility had ended a month ago, and Li Fei had been chosen as an honored concubine. So she would indeed see the emperor and hopefully, one day, she would give birth to his son. But that remained to be seen.

Meanwhile, Ling Xin thought of her cousin's true wish. She knew it hadn't been to grace the emperor's bed. She knew Li Fei had longed for someone else, a man from the north who was now dead. Life in the Forbidden City was her second choice, but she hoped that Li Fei had joy of it.

Ling Xin was about to suggest they go inside when Zhi Hao suddenly tensed. A half breath later, he spun her around behind him while she gasped in surprise. Then she saw what had startled him.

A red fox peered at them from beneath their tree bower. Bright eyes, thick red fur, and a swollen belly.

"Look at that," he murmured. "And here I thought you were the fox spirit."

"But do you see it?" she whispered, afraid of startling the creature. "Do you see her belly?"

"You think she's pregnant?" he asked. He tilted his head as he looked. "Maybe." He stepped forward, but the animal disappeared with a quick flick of her tail.

Ling Xin looked to see where the creature had gone. Together, they searched for her den, but found nothing. She seemed to be long gone.

"Don't tell Mama about her," Ling Xin said. "She thinks foxes are evil."

"Never," he said. "I could never doubt the creature who brought you tumbling into my arms."

She chuckled, remembering the frightening moment just before she fell off the wall and into his arms. "Let me tumble into your arms again," she said as she pulled him to their bedroom. "We can see how well you catch me."

He laughed as he followed her, and soon they were tumbling together, their laughter barely muffled out of respect for her parents. When they were done and Ling Xin laid spent in her husband's arms, her mind went back to the vixen.

She definitely thought the creature had been pregnant.

Could it be sign? She wondered as she rubbed a hand over her own thickening waist.

Yes, she decided. Yes, it was. The most auspicious sign of all.

NINE MONTHS LATER, their first son was born.

About the Author

A *USA Today* Bestseller, JADE LEE has been scripting love stories since she first picked up a set of paper dolls. Ball gowns and rakish lords caught her attention early (thank you Georgette Heyer), and her fascination with historical romance began. Author of more than 30 regency romances, Jade has a gift for creating a lively world, witty dialogue, and hot, sexy humor. Jade also writes contemporary and paranormal romance as Kathy Lyons. Together, they've won several industry awards, including the *Prism—Best of the Best, Romantic Times Reviewer's Choice,* and *Fresh Fiction's* Steamiest Read. Even though Kathy (and Jade) have written over 60 romance novels, she's just getting started. Check out her latest news at www.KathyLyons.com, Facebook: JadeLeeAuthor, and Twitter: JadeLeeAuthor. Instagram: KathyLyonsAuthor.